IN THE WINGS

IN THE WINGS
STORIES OF FORGOTTEN WOMEN

Edited by Bernadette Rule

Library and Archives Canada Cataloguing in Publication

In the wings : stories of forgotten women / editor, Bernadette Rule.

ISBN 978-1-927079-10-2

1. Short stories, Canadian (English). 2. Canadian fiction (English)-- 21st century. 3. Women–Fiction. I. Rule, Bernadette, 1951-

PS8323.W65I5 2012 C813'.01083522 C2012-905490-9

The publisher gratefully acknowledges the financial assistance of the Canada Council for the Arts.

Design and Typography: Rolf Busch

Published in 2012 by
Seraphim Editions
54 Bay Street
Woodstock, ON
Canada N4S 3K9

Second Printing 2012

Printed and Bound in Canada

CONTENTS

FOREWORD

It takes dedication and cooperation to omit women from the story of the human race. Not only do women outnumber men, but they are by definition central to the human race. So how is it that, by almost every account, women were essentially absent from all meetings, all conflicts, all conversations about how to proceed in any given society? Even this absence is rarely remarked upon in the history books, making it much more insidious than mere carelessness. *In the Wings* is an attempt to stop cooperating with this massive omission, to broaden our understanding of the past.

Some years ago I taught a course for the now defunct McMaster Writing Certificate program. I called the course Writing Women Characters, and the last assignment required the students to research a woman attached to a famous man, and then place her into a short story. The skill with which they imagined themselves into the lives of these "peripheral characters" delighted me, and I invited others to send me such stories. They have, in every case, been illuminating. Why, for example, is Ann Hathaway not remembered as Ann Shakespeare? Samuel de Champlain had a child bride shipped over from France? Oscar Wilde and Somerset Maugham had wives?

This collection invites you to enter the world of Louis Riel, Charles Dickens, Walt Disney and others through the women who inspired and cared for them. This fresh perspective will surprise you. These stories give us insight, not only into the women themselves, but also into the men to whom they are connected, and into the times and places in which they lived. *In the Wings* also re-examines the lives of a few women we think we know. It takes Laura Secord off the candy box lid, and shows us what happened to the first person to go over Niagara Falls in a barrel – a woman, yes. This anthology not only informs and entertains, it challenges our ideas about how a society shapes a sense of itself.

The fifteen stories in the book are followed by two essays: "The Rani of Jhansi, 'Bravest of the Rebels'" and "An Unremarkable Life?" The first is about an Indian queen, Rani Lakshmibai, who became caught up in the Rebellion of 1857 and died fighting in it. The other is about the writer's grandmother, Bertha Fried Hirning, a pioneer in Alberta's Peace River country. These essays prompt even more questions about how and why some are remembered, and some are forgotten.

A print-on-demand booklet designed primarily, but not exclusively, for teachers is also available, for those who wish to delve further, or use *In the Wings* as a textbook. The supplement includes three chapters about literary genres – fiction, non-fiction and the increasingly blurred line between them – bibliographies and acknowledgements by the authors, comprehension questions for each story, and essay ideas for students. To order the booklet please contact the publisher.

Even in those societies in which women have been oppressed and kept from exercising any kind of power but sexual power, the female perspective is worth considering. It is the other half of the story. The writers of this anthology and I hope that *In the Wings* introduces you to people you've never heard of, and broadens your perspective on people you've never thought about. We hope it helps give voice to the still largely untold side of the story of human history.

Bernadette Rule

A PAIR OF GLOVES

Linda Helson

He didn't look like a genius, not then – it were only later they called him that – and who knows what a genius looks like anyway. At the edge of the garden he stood, as I draped the linens over the bushes in mid-November. I saw him there out of the corner of my eye, just watching in that way he had. Ordinary enough, a little skinny, I thought, a little narrow in the leg. A boy really. Up to no good, I thought, having the freedom to stand around at butchering season when there were plenty of work to be done.

I may have flirted a bit, I admit that. I don't know what got into me, in my condition. He looked such easy prey. A glance up at him and away again, a little more sway in my walk as I moved, a stretch that showed my bosom to advantage as I stood up from the basket. Not too much of a stretch. I didn't want any hint of my belly showing.

It was the stretch that did it though. Suddenly I were on my knees puking into the grass, trying to miss the edge of the sheet spread out there.

He were through the gate instantly and kneeling beside me, holding my hair back from my face and uttering soft and soothing sounds as I heaved my guts. I could feel tears prick my eyes, it were so rare for someone to act kindly toward me then. Kindness wouldn't last when the baby came. Then I'd be known for the wanton I was.

When I finished puking, he helped me to my feet and pulled a rag from his pocket to wipe my mouth. He held my chin firmly in his hand and I had to look up at him. He smiled. The tears threatened to spill over then and I had to blink furiously to hold them back.

"Don't fret yourself, lass. It's going to be all right."

That's when I saw the gloves, tucked into the waist of his leggings, and I knew – Uncle had sold me. That's what all that whispered talk between Mam and him had been. Unseen in the shed, I milked Bess whilst they went at it outside in the yard. I could sniff the tenor of the conversation but not taste the meat, as they argued back and forth.

I'd had to confess to Mam. She would have spotted it soon enough. She lamented up and down the room about a girl not having a father to protect her and what would become of me and the stain on the family name and much more besides. Then she hugged me close and cossetted me and we had a good cry together, while she thought what might be done. She told Uncle about my condition. He give me a right old beating. I still had the bruises from it. At last Mam stopped him, but he called me some vicious names I'll not soon forget.

I guess he got busy then. This being the result – a ne'er-do-well boy with the reputation of a dreamer. But kind, as he'd just shown.

I sighed. At least he were from a respectable family. So he should be. I had a substantial inheritance portion, according to Pa's will, to be payed on my marriage day. Still – a boy. And me twenty-six, a woman grown, and more. Why would he agree to this? I'd heard his father had fallen on hard times. Could that be it? No prospect of following in his father's business? But what did he know of farming?

The gloves were his engagement gift. When I accepted them we had a contract, unspoken but clear. And what could I do, puking all the time, beginning to show, no other prospects about, and no idea who the father was? It wasn't what I'd dreamed of, but the time for dreaming had passed.

He said he made the gloves himself. They were remarkable. Soft doeskin with fine stitches all round and decorative embroidery, our initials – AH and WS – twined on the gauntlets I later discovered, when I had the leisure to study them closely. A little tight on my hands, as they had swelled with the pregnancy, but I thought the gloves would fit well later. A fine gift – they eased my burden a little.

We had to get a special license. No time for the banns to be read thrice, as Advent were almost upon us and I could not wait until Epiphany. We were married at St. Mary's, Temple Groton, as it were out of the way. The date: November 30, three months and six days after the rape.

That happened at the St. Bartholemew's Day Fair in Stratford. I don't remember much about it, just trying to push the men away – to no avail. There were three of them, two to hold me down, with my skirt tossed over my head so I couldn't see them, while each one took his turn. I do remember the first one hurt me the most, as my maidenhead broke. I heard his exclamation of surprise.

One of the men holding my arms said, "Well, the deed's done now." And they continued their grunting and shoving at me.

I must have passed out. I awoke alone in a field in the early morning, all messy and sticky. Before dragging myself home, I tried to clean up by stripping down and sinking into the river at a discreet spot. Of course, in the country you never know who might be watching. I'd heard that cold water could prevent a pregnancy, but 'twas August. The Avon was warm.

The next day proved a trial, trying to pretend nothing untoward had happened and praying all day to Mary and all the saints while I went about my chores. I thought She might have been sympathetic, having endured the same shame herself. But it certainly warn't God's messenger who'd visited me that summer night.

You'd think I would know better at my age, but I blame the novelty of the travelling players. I'd been transported by their dramas and payed little attention to the number of drinks the men plyed me with. I let myself be flattered by their attentions to me and was curious when they offered to show me behind the scenes.

By that time I'd got dizzy with the drink. When I stumbled, one of them caught me and held me up, one arm about me and one hand planted on my breast. I tried to move away from him, but another put his hands on my laces and began to loosen them. I felt frightened, but I enjoyed the sensations in my breasts, too. Pa had kept me on a tight rein, but he had died a year ago. I missed him, yet this summer I'd felt my first taste of freedom. Mam were too distracted in her grief to pay much attention to me, so long as my chores got done. She relied on me to watch over the other children and set an example. What an example.

With Pa gone, we had a lot more work to keep up and it were hard on us. The farm workers didn't attend to women's orders nor my young brothers' the way they had Pa's. Uncle hired us an overseer, Jem, a self-important and stupid man, but at least the other men obeyed him.

We got the planting done and the harvest in.

Jem let me know he were available in the hayloft any time I had the inclination. I did feel curious, but I knew he'd a wife and three little ones off near Bishop's Stortford, so I stayed away from him.

All my precautions come to nothing, though, at the Bartholemew Fair. As the eldest, I'd taken some of the flock in to Stratford to sell. One of the men come along to protect me, but he met some of his cronies and went off drinking with them, saying to me, "You'll be safe enough watching the pageant, lass, and I'll come get you later."

I didn't relish walking back along the path to Shottery with a drunken loon after dark, but what were I to do? I don't know if he ever did come looking for me. I never asked him. I were too ashamed. I might have been safe with him, and if not, at least I'd know the name of my babe's father.

She were born late May and we called her Susanna, a name popular among the Puritans. In our position, it were wise, Will said, to appear to have Protestant leanings.

Will made a lusty young lover, I'll say that for him – after all, he were just eighteen – and quite imaginative as well, whispering Latin poetry into my ear as he explored my body with his hands. He called me "his best bed" as he lay on top of me out in the fields, sated after his exploits, or in the feather bed in the room allotted to us in his parents' house.

In one of those quiet times, I screwed up my courage and asked him why he had agreed to marry me. He told me he'd watched as the players seduced me at Bartholemew Fair. Watched, and done nothing.

"What could a lad have done against three grown men?" I asked. He shrugged, but his eyes were flinty.

"When I heard you were with child and that your uncle was casting about for a husband for you, I let it be known I was willing."

"What of Anne Whately then?" By that time I'd heard the gossip, that he had gone to Farmer Whately and withdrawn his suit.

"She'll be all right. Her father has a good farm. She won't lack for offers … I could have stopped those men, Anne, but I didn't. You're my responsibility."

I let it lie then. Why look a gift horse in the mouth? My father had had a good farm too, yet here was I, married to a boy.

With the birth of the twins things changed. Susanna had been a content baby, pliable and happy. With Judith and Hamnet everything were different. To start with there were two of them and they seemed always to be hungry, always competing for my attention. Hamnet were a sickly child, and Judith fractious. Once they were crawling, they were everywhere underfoot, and the house echoed with their wailing.

I thought I should go mad with the noise and the crowded rooms, with his father looming and his mother disapproving of my country ways (as if she weren't country born herself) and the reek of skins being treated in the workshop, the smell invading everything. His father's business were thriving again, but Will seemed uninterested – "not pulling his weight" as his father constantly complained. "A few years of schooling don't make you so fine you can't learn a trade, lad."

But more and more Will was from home. More and more I felt it must be my fault. By now I'd passed thirty and bearing the twins had thickened and spread my body. There were no more frisking in the fields under the moonlight with Will, and little enough in our own bed. He often slipped from between the sheets in the night to creep back in the pre-dawn hours and press his cold body against mine under the blankets. But it were just for warmth.

I guessed he had a young lover. I hoped she wouldn't come to grief as I had done. Surely he'd take care. I felt I couldn't confront him with my suspicion, given the debt I owed him, so I let things slide, drifting further apart from him, praying his affection would return to me somehow. I didn't see as I could do much else.

It took me by surprise when the Squire accused him of poaching. No wonder the kettle were never short of venison, and his father rich in fine doe skins. When John came at him as a ne'er-do-well, Will stood stubborn.

"You were happy enough to have the skins and not ask closely," he replied to his father's charges.

Then one day Will took off. The Squire were making it too hot for him hereabouts. "I'll hide out with the players for a bit. Travel around. Maybe see London," he'd whispered to me in the night before he slipped away. "Keep my best bed safe."

We heard nothing for five long years and then word come from London. Will were living in Bishopsgate, doing whatever turned up, sometimes acting and writing parts for the players at The Theatre.

Ironic, to be sure. I wondered if he were friends with the very men who had used me. But it were just a passing thought. I felt glad to learn of his safe landing.

Money began to arrive from him, at first in dribs and drabs, but then in larger sums. One day he arrived in Stratford announcing he had bought New Place in Chapel Court from Mr. Underhill. I was that flummoxed. In the ten years he'd been in London Will had done well for himself, and for us. At last I'd be able to move out of the Shakespeare's residence and into a spacious house of my own. The joy of it! Though by that time there were scarcely any need for all those rooms. The girls had grown up and Hamnet were six years dead, poor mite. He'd never been strong.

They say, after Hamnet's death Will wrote his greatest plays, working out his grief in words on a page. I have to believe them. I never saw one performed.

At Lent, or whenever the plague closed the theatres, or when winter clutched the land, as it did in those years with a brutality unheard of in living memory, Will would appear at the door of our new house. He always had ideas for improvements and the money to make them.

When the old queen died, Will's company came under the patronage of the Scotch king, James; now they were The King's Men.

By then we were rich beyond anything I'd ever dreamt of. Will held shares in The Globe, in the company, had investments, enjoyed the patronage of the king – and all from his genius at making up stories and characters for the stage. A miracle, to be sure.

When The Globe burnt to the ground – an accident that come about when a cannon were fired off during a performance of *Henry VIII* and set fire to the roof thatch – Will come home for good. He said he'd had enough of London, enough of currying favour with the nobility, enough of sitting up late with stubs of candles burning while he penned words onto parchment, enough of frozen ink in winter and the stench of the streets in summer. He wanted country air and space.

He were worn out, and nearing fifty. The years of worrying how each new play would be received, of irregular hours and tavern meals, too much drinking and rich foods had taken their toll. Now fat and bald, Will were content to sit by the fire and read his Ovid once again in quiet.

When he died, after a night of carousing with some of his theatre cronies who had come to Stratford to visit him, I weren't surprised. He had made out his will a few weeks before, leaving everything to Susanna in trust for her male offspring. For some reason Will had never taken to Judith, his own daughter. To me he left the "second best bed", a joke that only he and I shared. To the last he had a fine sense of humour – a genius for it, people said.

As I stared at his dead body, I thought back over thirty years and more. It weren't much of a marriage, not after the first few years, not after he went to London. He'd been a restless youth with fine sensibilities, but felt hampered by the realities of married life. He craved excitement. He was a good provider though. We were so rich, he could afford to be buried inside Trinity Church, not out in the graveyard.

I wore the gloves he'd given me as an engagement present to his funeral. I'd not had much occasion to wear such grand garments over the years so they were like new. They were a tight fit as I knew they would be, but they seemed appropriate.

Author's Note

I belong to a women's writing group that meets once a month at members' homes. Each month the host assigns a topic for the next month's meeting. One month the topic was, "he didn't look like a genius" or "something to do with genius". Almost immediately Anne began to talk to me.

I was well into the story before I thought that I had better check my facts. I had taught Shakespeare in high school and had visited Stratford-on-Avon a few times, but I needed to check the dates of the children's births. When I did the math I realized that Anne must have become pregnant with Susanna, her first child, on St. Bartholomew's Day, a time of much festivity in Elizabethan England.

The rape is fiction. She and Will could just as easily have become drunk and headed for the fields. In fact, that is probably what happened. In any case, none of his biographers seems to have picked up on St. Bartholomew's Day.

I also did some reading in a wonderful book that had been gathering dust on my shelf for years: Samuel Schoenbaum's *William Shakespeare: A Documentary Life.* I checked the internet for the various portraits that are claimed to be of Shakespeare. The chubby statue of him that surmounts his grave had always bothered me; now that I have written this story it makes sense. He was wealthy; he could afford to eat well.

I adjusted what I had written to fit the facts I found, and Anne just kept talking.

TELL ME A STORY (DITES-MOI UNE HISTOIRE)

Michelle Ward-Kantor

New France, 1624

The women sat on the ground, drinking berry mint tea. They had just eaten a satisfying meal of stewed moose, which they had carried with them for the berry-gathering trek they were on.

"We have done well," said Shanut. "One more day and we will have enough uishatshimina and inniminana to last several weeks."

The women began to prepare their camp for sleeping, spreading out the furs they had brought. Hélène was slightly nervous about being here, as there had been talk of enemy bands in the area. But her friends had reassured her and she had wanted to come with them, as this was the last time she would ever take part in this task.

After preparing their beds, the women knelt with Hélène, as had become their custom when they were together. She did not ask, "To which God do you pray?" Her hands found the hands of the women on either side of her and she clasped them firmly, heartened by their warmth. She closed her eyes and prayed for their safe return from this journey.

After the prayer circle ended, Anishen came and sat beside Hélène, as she often did after praying. "Did you bring your book? Tipishkau-pishum is bright enough to read by tonight."

Hélène smiled. "Oui, la lune est belle. Non, I did not bring my book. It was extra weight that I didn't need to carry. I suppose I have enough trouble carrying what I must."

"Well, then, Tuta tipatshimun. Dites-moi une histoire."

Hélène smiled at Anishen and told her how God had helped her when she had first come to this wild place. "I felt so alone at first and missed my home so much. Ce premier hiver, était si terrible, obscure et froid. Monsieur Champlain was away so much. The few men at the settlement are no substitute for women friends. God answered my prayers when you and your sisters arrived at the settlement that first spring, after returning from your winter home."

Anishen laughed, remembering. "Your clothing was so fine! Ah, but you don't always wear your fine clothing now."

Hélène ran her hand over the buckskin boots that Anishen had given her. "These are better, more practical for hikes in the woods."

The sisters and Hélène talked quietly, until they fell asleep, snug under their furs.

The next day was quiet, with a still blue sky. The women carried their belongings on their backs. Hélène's load was the lightest. The others had insisted she was not used to these journeys and a heavy load would tire her too much.

"How many weeks before you must leave?" Shanut spoke into the quiet, as the women trudged slowly along.

"Nishtu. Although I love you all, I guess it is time to go home. J'ai maintenant vécu ici quatre ans. It seems like much longer somehow."

"We will miss you, fine dresser." Anishen came up beside Hélène and touched her arm. "Soon there will be no one to read us French tales and no one to tell us of your God."

Hélène squeezed Anishen's hand. "For me, there will be no one who can prepare moose so the taste is just tangy enough. Of course, there will be no moose at all."

The others laughed with Hélène.

"And who will brush my hair, and hold the mirror for me to look into?" Anishen teased back.

When Hélène arrived, the young girls had been fascinated with Hélène's mahogany-handled mirror. They took turns looking at themselves in it, touching their noses, eyes, mouths, as if they could not believe the parts belonged to them. Even now, they never seemed to tire of looking into it.

"Tell us again about this place, the one with les marchés and clothes made of ... what do you call that?"

"Do you mean satin?" Hélène answered.

"Niihiiy, satin, like the green dress you sometimes wear."

Hélène reached up to stroke the intricate beads Anishen had given her for her 24th birthday. "Paris seems like a strange memory to me now. It haunts me in my sleep. Sometimes I dream of the parlor where I used to sit with my mother in the mornings, with the warm light all around us. I miss Maman so much."

"What about your husband, Monsieur Champlain? Will you also miss him?"

"I see little of him now as it is. Anyway, perhaps he is more of a father to me than a husband," Hélène said.

"A father! That's no fun for certain activities, is it!" Matinen and Anishen laughed.

Hélène blushed. "Girls! Ce n'est pas approprié."

Anishen, several steps ahead of Hélène, stopped suddenly. She had been looking through a break in the trees and she put her arm out to stop the others. Hélène paused, her feet planted one step ahead of the other. She breathed in the fir tree scent around her, saw the bright indigo sky between the trees. Through her buckskin shoes, her feet caressed the ground, feeling the shape of the earth, this land her friends called Great Turtle Island.

"I am going ahead to check something," said Anishen, so quietly the others had to strain to hear her. She motioned for Shanut to follow her. "We will be back soon. If we are not, turn around and go back to the settlement."

Hélène also stood to follow, but Matinen pulled her back down. Matinen always listened to Anishen, for Anishen was the eldest. Hélène and Matinen waited in the trees until the sun's shadow moved across the rock they were leaning against. Then Matinen stood up and peeked through the trees. "Come," she said abruptly. "We must go back."

"Go back? We can't leave them here." Hélène felt a slight panic. "Is it an Iroquois camp? Is that what you have seen?" She began to walk forward.

Matinen took Hélène's hand. "Hurry, Hélène. We must go."

Hélène had heard stories of the powerful Iroquois nation. Some of the young native men she had known at the settlement had gone out to practice their warring techniques, and had not returned. There were stories of captives being tortured, even eaten. Her skin tingled with the adrenaline rush that started in her middle and spread outward into her limbs. She thought she might be sick with fear.

Anishen and Shanut did not return. Two weeks after Hélène and Matinen had returned to the settlement without them, Matinen and her family departed for their winter home. Hélène watched as Matinen's family stoically boarded their canoes for the journey up the St. Lawrence River.

"Perhaps we will find my sisters. They cannot be far," said Matinen hopefully.

"Au revoir, mon amie. Please take this for you and your sisters; I pray that God will bring you safely together. I will never forget you." Hélène hugged Matinen and placed a bundle in her hand.

"Aiame, uitsheuakanimau." Matinen wiped tears from her eyes.

The space in the camp was quiet then, her friends' laughter heard only in Hélène's dreams. Hélène took that quiet space with her across the sea to her home, along with nightmares about the Iroquois. She took the smell of roasted moose, the taste of fresh blueberries, and the feel of woven baskets beneath her hands. She took the songs of the blue-jays, the glimpses of deer and the feel of the hot sun on her face. She took the story of Great Turtle Island, told to her when she first arrived. She left behind the book she frequently read from, her satin dresses and the mirror with the mahogany handle.

The nun felt her heart twist. She recalled a young girl with black hair and long pecan limbs, a woman with a smile that pulled up higher on one corner of her mouth than the other in a lopsided grin. "You said your mother did not always have the name Kahentawaks. What name did she used to have?" she asked quietly, hopefully.

"Kahentawaks was a Mohawk name given to her at the mid-winter ceremony, just as Konwakeri was given hers. The name given my mother by her own people was Anishen. My aunt was called Shanut."

At the sound of these names, the nun clasped her hands together. She brought them to her mouth, bit on her knuckle to stem the emotions that sprang up inside her. Then she leaned forward and grasped her visitor's hands once again. "May I see your necklace, child?"

The young woman took it from around her neck, and handed it to the nun, who received it as reverently as if it had been a rosary. She looked closely at the shells made into delicate beads, at the long unusual piece of wood, with its markings and special curves. She looked for a long time, and saw that the wood was mahogany. And the tears gathered in her eyes and spilled down her cheeks, tears that she had kept inside all these long years, tears that even God, in the comfort of this convent, had not been able to fully heal.

Sister Hélène stood and hugged Wanik to her heart.

Author's Note

Hélène Boullé married Samuel de Champlain in 1610 at the age of 12. Champlain was in his early 40's. Hélène came from a wealthy Parisian family and Champlain used some of the dowry from this marriage to finance his colony in New France. Hélène accompanied him to present day Quebec City in 1620 and returned to Paris in 1624. As her husband was often away, traveling between France and the colony in New France, Hélène was on her own. The only European woman living there at that time was Marie Rollet and it has been suggested that the women were not very friendly towards each other, perhaps because of different beliefs.

Hélène spent much of her time with the native people, most likely the Montagnais and possibly, the Hurons. Hélène missed cosmopolitan Paris, although she spent her time teaching and reading to the natives and learning some of their language, most likely Montagnais-Innu. The natives, in turn, were taken with her fine clothing and elegant manners.

Hélène, raised in a Calvinist home, converted to Catholicism two years after marrying Champlain. After returning to Paris, she became estranged from Champlain, who died in 1635. Hélène, always very religious, entered the convent of Meaux in 1648, which she financed with her own money. She died in 1654 at the age of 56.

From 1620-24, there was unrest between the Algonquin and Iroquois nations. If another tribe did capture women and/or children, it was not uncommon for them to be taken as slaves or adopted by the tribe.

A word on the Innu language ...

There are five dialects of innu-aimun spoken by present-day Innu, two in Labrador and three in Quebec. Currently, a project is underway by the University of Newfoundland to codify the spelling system of these dialects. Part of this fascinating dictionary is available at www.innu-aimun.ca; however, the Quebec Innu dictionary is not yet finished. I have tried to be consistent and use what is called Montagnais-Innu, finding the information on other web-sites listed at the end of this story.

Although the native women in this story are fictional, I wanted to give them names that would have truly represented the Innu and

Mohawk (Kanieǹkeha) peoples. However, in the course of my research, I discovered that traditional names are difficult, if not impossible, to find. Naming ceremonies are very important and spiritual in nature. Names are given by the clan mother, and in traditional times, a person had a name like no other, one that was meant only for that person. These names are not widely available to non-native people. Therefore, some of the names I have used are translations of Christian names, ones that may or may not have been used in the 1600s.

Glossary of Terms – (in order of appearance in story)

Innu-aimun

Uishatshimina – red berries

Inniminana – blueberries

Tipishkau-pishum – moon

Tuta tipatshimun – Make up a story.

Nishtu – three

Niihiiy – yes

Aiame, uitsheuakanimau – Goodbye friend.

French

Oui, la lune est beau. – Yes, the moon is beautiful.

Dites-moi une histoire. – Tell me a story.

Ce primier hiver, était si terrible, obscure et froid. – That first winter was terrible, so dark and cold.

J'ai maintenant vécu ici quatre ans. – I have lived here four years now.

les marchés – markets

Ce n'est pas approprié – What you have said is not appropriate.

Au revoir, mon amie. – Goodbye my friend.

Mon épouse est très résiliente. – My wife is very resilient.

I would like to acknowledge Professor Cornelius Jaenen, Professor Emeritus at the University of Ottawa for answering my questions, including what Algonkian language Hélène may have learned to speak.

Books and Web-site Information

Bonvillain, Nancy. Indians of North America: The Mohawk. Chelsea House Publishers. New York: 1992.

Conrad, Margaret, Alvin Finkel and Cornelius Jaenen, History of the Canadian Peoples-Beginnings to 1867, Copp Clark Pitman Ltd., Toronto: 1993.

Gillmor, Don and Pierre Turgeon, Canada: A People's History – Volume One, McClelland & Stewart Ltd., Toronto: 2000.

Canadian History: A Distinctive Viewpoint, by D. Garneau
www.telusplanet.net/public/dgarneau/french12.htm

Canadian National Archives
www.lcbp.org/PDFs/MadameChamplain.pdf
www.geocities.com/bigorrin/innu_kids.htm

Innu stories from the land. Virtual Museum Canada: 2005.
www.tipatshimuna.ca

IPL (Internet Public Library) Kidspace: Say Hello to the World, Regents of University of Michigan, 2007.
(**website no longer accessible)
www.kahonwes.com/language/mohawk

www.monsite.wanadoo.fr/champlain-and-co
(**website no longer accessible)
This site was translated from French by translate.google.com

Minister of Public Works and Government Services, Minister of Indian Affairs and Northern Development, Ottawa, 2000
www.ainc-inac.gc.ca

Public records of Canada
www.home.comcast.net/~samuel.de.champlain

Redish Laura and Orrin Lewis, Native Languages of America.
www.native-languages.org

Teya Peya Productions, Canada – A Canadian Arts, Education and Entertainment Company (a company created by "indigenous peoples")
www.shannonthunderbird.com/indigenous_history.htm

KONEWATSI'TSIAIÉNNI AND THE GOVERNOR'S LADY

Jean Rae Baxter

THE PAIN HIT SUDDENLY, WITH TIGHTNESS IN MY CHEST, and all at once every ounce of air tried to escape my body. This had happened to me before. Many times.

"Mama!" Miriam screamed, catching me in her arms as I folded to the floor. She helped me to the rocking chair beside the kitchen fire. Unable to stand, I resigned myself to leaning back and looking up at her. After a few minutes the pain stopped, leaving me dizzy and sweaty.

"You need rest," Miriam said, "weeks of rest."

I shook my head. As soon as I could speak, I said, "I want to go home. Book me passage on the next boat to Kingston. I can rest on the journey. When Death comes for me, I want to be under my own roof."

Her eyes brimmed with tears. "Mama, make your home with me. Please stay in Niagara, where I can care for you." In her voice I heard the fear – the knowledge – that if I left, she would never see me again.

"Back in Kingston," I said, "your sister can look after me. There'll be three pairs of hands to share the burden of caring for a useless old woman. Miriam saw the practicality of my returning home, and also understood the strength of my desire.

Upon going down to the harbour to enquire, Miriam learned that the *Mississaga* was due to sail from Niagara in one week, on September 13. But when she tried to book my passage, the harbour master told her that all passenger space had been reserved for Lieutenant Governor Simcoe, his wife and children, and their servants.

"Tell them it's Molly Brant who needs a berth," Miriam said. "I'm not leaving until you do."

When this information reached Mrs. Simcoe, she herself ordered that a cabin be provided for me.

Miriam returned triumphant from the harbour, a ticket in her hand and her dark eyes flashing. Those dark eyes are the only feature she got from me. In every other way she takes after her father. In appearance, she is the least Indian of my children.

After a week of rest, I was able to walk without assistance up the *Mississaga's* gangway. It was the evening of September 12. Mrs. Simcoe was already on board. Although the boat was not due to sail until the next morning, it was important to be ready for a favourable wind whenever it arose. On deck a little girl and a little boy, both neatly dressed, stood watching the loading under the careful eye of their nursemaid. Those must be the Simcoe children, I thought, for I had heard that the Governor and Mrs. Simcoe had brought their two youngest to Upper Canada, while their four older girls remained in England with relatives until their father's term as governor was completed.

In the evening, while we were still moored, Mrs. Simcoe visited my cabin. It was an honour to be waited upon by the Governor's lady. I have received, of late, many honours.

Mrs. Simcoe was a small woman with sharp, dark eyes, a tiny face, and a strong, determined chin. She sat down on a chair that was bolted to the floor and regarded me fixedly as I lay back upon my cushions. After inquiring about my health, she made no effort to conceal her curiosity about my life.

She mentioned that she and the Governor had dined with Captain Brant, as she called my brother, and found him to be a charming and most interesting dinner companion. Through her praise, she found the surest way to my confidence. When she asked about my childhood, I told her that I had been born in 1736, or so I believed, for we Mohawk count the years, but do not give them names or numbers. My brother Thayendanegea, I said, was born six years later.

"We lived near Canajoharie in the Mohawk Valley. Our father died while we were young children. After his death, our mother remarried. Our stepfather's name was Nickus Brant."

"So you took your stepfather's name. Was he a white man?"

"No. He was Mohawk, a sachem of the Turtle clan, but he told us that his father's father had been Dutch. Mother wanted us to take his name. She saw that the world was changing, and wanted her children to be ready. That was why she sent us to the mission school. When we enrolled, they gave my brother the name Joseph. They named me Mary, though everyone called me Molly even then. I did not like my new name, but I got used to it. Only my Mohawk name has power for me."

"And what is that?"

"Konwatsi'tsiaiénni."

"Heavens!" Mrs. Simcoe exclaimed. "I couldn't pronounce that, let alone spell it."

"My name means that someone lends me a flower. It is a lovely name. I tried to persuade Sir William to call me Konwatsi'tsiaiénni, but he said Molly was more to his taste."

At the mention of my husband, Mrs. Simcoe's ears pricked up. I was accustomed to that reaction. People have always been curious about our marriage – who could blame them? But I had said as much as I wanted to. After a few minutes, with apologies for tiring me, Mrs. Simcoe took her leave.

Today I am a respectable woman, fifty-nine years old, the relict of Sir William Johnson, First Baronet of New York. I take pride in that, but do not think for a minute that Sir William raised me up in the world. My family holds high rank among the Mohawk people.

When Sir William first met me, I'm sure he had no idea that we would remain together as long as he lived. But he saw from the start how I might become useful to him.

When I was still a girl, the Mohawk Elders thought I had the potential to become a Clan Mother. As part of my training for this role, they sent me when I was eighteen with a delegation to Philadelphia to complain to the authorities about fraudulent land transfers. An interesting experience for me. The English authorities handled it wisely, once it was explained to them that no one, not even a chief, possessed the authority to sell communal land. The Mohawk elders won a victory there, and I returned to my village knowing something about diplomacy.

But at that age, I was still a wild thing. What I cared about were fast horses and my freedom. When I reached the age of twenty-two, I still had not met a man I liked enough to marry.

It was a horse that brought me to Sir William's notice. I was with friends visiting Fort Johnson, which was not so much a fort as a fortified house. Sir William, as Superintendent of Indian Affairs, kept open house for Indians as well as whites. Mohawks were always welcome there.

On this particular day, several young officers were riding about on the field in front of the fort, showing off their horses' paces. Sir William was present, but I hardly noticed him. At forty-three, he was too old to interest me. The creature that caught my eye was a big bay gelding.

It embarrasses me to remember how I called out to the officer astride the horse as he cantered by, "Give me a ride!"

"With pleasure," he said, and reined in the bay.

With one leap, I was seated behind the rider, and we galloped all around the field, my braids and the fringes of my tunic flying.

When the ride ended, Sir William was livid.

"Take that horse to the stable and cool it down," he said to the young officer. "Remember in future that you are a gentleman, and govern yourself accordingly."

I had jumped down quickly and was striding off with as much dignity as I could muster when Sir William called out, "Just a minute, young woman."

I halted. Nobody disobeyed Sir William.

"Who are you?"

"I'm *Konwatsi'tsiaiénni*," I said. I held my chin up and looked him straight in the eye so he would know that we were equals. "But you may call me Molly Brant."

As his eyes locked on mine, I kept my face as stiff as a wooden mask, the way I'd been brought up to do in the face of any challenge. For a minute, neither of us spoke. Gradually his expression softened from anger to amusement. He smiled.

"You pounced like a wildcat upon that horse's back. What else can you do, besides ride horses?"

I was sure he would not care whether I could bead a moccasin or paddle a canoe, so I told him that I knew my letters and numbers, from having attended the mission school.

"I need someone to keep my books," he said. "Do you seek employment?"

The offer was so unexpected that I had no time to think. Keeping books did not sound difficult. White people "kept" chickens and pigs, creatures that had to be fed and kept confined. That might be hard work. But books do not eat, nor do they try to escape.

Always eager to try something new, I replied, "I can do that."

"Come with me," he said. Sir William took me into the house. When he opened the door to the dark little office he called his counting room, I had the feeling that I was about to cross into the unknown.

Sir William opened a ledger that rested on a stand and explained what I would have to do. Quickly I realized that keeping books meant writing down what you spent and what you earned. At the mission school I had learned to add and subtract, which appeared to be all the arithmetic a bookkeeper needed.

We agreed upon a salary of twenty pounds a year, in addition to my room and board. He promised that I would not be housed like an indentured servant or a slave. I was to have a room of my own with a feather bed.

I did not like the way Sir William's eyes lingered upon my body when he mentioned the feather bed. His reputation was well known. He had sired bastards all over the county, showing no preference for white women over Indians. Yet I believed that I would be safe from his advances, for he had his mistress already living at Fort Johnson, a big-bosomed German named Catherine Weissenberg, who had already borne him three children. Sir William unashamedly acknowledged these little ones, Nancy, Polly and John, as part of his household.

Having no desire to become a second mistress, I maintained an air of dignity on all occasions, especially when alone with Sir William. From time to time, I reminded him that my rank was high among the Mohawk people. He knew this. My influence among my people was one reason he valued me. For, as Superintendent of Indian Affairs, his first duty was to maintain good relations with the Mohawks, as with all the Six Nations of the Iroquois Confederacy.

Increasingly he consulted me about one issue or another. I remember the time he asked what I thought was my people's greatest need.

"Most of my people consider it to be secure possession of our lands," I answered. "But in my opinion, education is as great a need."

"More mission schools?" he asked.

"That's a start. But I meant higher education, to fit us for business and diplomacy. Look at my brother Thayendanegea. Is he not as clever as your son John? With the same education, could he not also become a man of power and influence?" This John, Sir William's legitimate son, was his heir.

"Possibly," Sir William said. "Your brother is a likely lad."

Sir William did not mention the subject again. But I noticed that he kept an eye on my brother, who frequently visited Fort Johnson. Though only sixteen, Thayendanegea was handsome and well-spoken. He was also clever and ambitious.

I was not surprised when, two years later, Sir William sent my brother away to school in Connecticut. He could see that Joseph, as Sir William insisted on calling him, had talents far beyond those needed for hunting and for war.

The *Mississaga* weighed anchor at six in the morning, and we passed a rough day, sailing into a strong headwind. I remained in my cabin, fully dressed but lying on my berth, having promised Miriam that I would rest on the two-day voyage. Late in the afternoon Mrs. Simcoe came to see me.

"I find that remaining on deck keeps me from becoming seasick," she said. "It is only the desire to see how you fare that has brought me below."

She sat down and, tilting her head, gave me an appraising look. I had changed from the plain, black gown I had worn the previous day to one of fine, dark blue wool with deep silken fringes across the yoke and along the sleeves.

"I admire your style of dress," she said. "It suits you well."

"Thank you. Sir William also approved. He wanted me to wear the finest silks, satins and velvets, but I always insisted upon fringes. To me, clothes without fringes do not look complete."

Mrs. Simcoe smiled as her hands smoothed the skirt of her pale grey gown. "I must speak to my dressmaker about the addition of fringes. When I return to England, I might introduce a new fashion." She rose. "Now that I know you are well, I shall return to my cabin to write in my diary. I make an entry every day, if possible. Someday I intend to publish my diary as a book." Before opening the door, she turned toward me. "Miss Molly, have you ever thought to keep a diary?"

"Me?" I laughed.

"You could do it. There are many who would love to read about your life."

After she had gone, her words remained with me. She was right. But I would never seek to publish the story of my life. My memories are locked in my heart, and there they shall remain.

There I was, a Mohawk maiden living under the same roof as Sir William Johnson, to say nothing of Catherine Weissenberg and their three children. It was obvious that Sir William admired me. I was pretty, with fine features, smooth skin, and a graceful figure. Had I made myself available, he would gladly have taken me as a second mistress.

Catherine must have suspected this, for she did not befriend me. In fact, she seldom spoke to me and was never in my presence if she could avoid it.

As time went by, Sir William seemed less old to me, especially when he took off the long white wig that he wore in public. His natural hair was dark and hardly touched with grey. But I was determined to be his bookkeeper and not his concubine. Thus I avoided giving him smiles that he might mistake for invitations, and I always conducted myself with decorum. No more leaping onto horses' backs for me.

Then Catherine died. She had cut her finger slicing potatoes. The cut became infected. Within a week, blood poisoning killed her, leaving Sir William stunned.

I had never felt that he loved her deeply. She was a servant, below him in social class. If he cared for her, it was to the same degree that he cared for his dogs. But to have her so suddenly struck down, a woman in her prime, leaving three small children! Only a heart of stone would not be moved.

Her funeral was small, attended by her children, the household staff (including me) and Sir William. Afterwards, I chanced to enter the counting room to complete certain entries in the ledger, and there was Sir William sitting by the fire. The room was small, dark and private. Probably he had not expected his solitude to be disturbed. When he raised his head, I saw tears in his eyes.

This was no time to stand on ceremony. Instead of excusing myself and withdrawing, I pulled up a chair and sat beside him.

"Truly, sir, I am sorry for your loss," I said.

He reached out to take my hand. I did not pull it away.

"Miss Molly," he said, "Catherine was loyal and obedient and she lived only to please me. I fear that she received little in return."

I did not answer. We sat there by the fire, my hand in his, for perhaps half an hour until a servant brought word that two officers had come to call. My sympathy must have touched him, as his remorse had touched me.

"You do me good, Miss Molly," he said as he left to greet his guests.

I made no entries in the ledger that afternoon, but took Nancy, Polly and John for a walk along the river. It was a fine spring day. We brought with us one of Sir William's beagles. The children threw sticks for the dog, and their spirits seemed brighter from the exercise.

Upon our return, Sir William invited me to join the company for dinner. This surprised me, for Catherine had never dined with Sir William's guests. I sensed that something new was about to begin.

That night he came to my bed, quietly opening the bed curtains, slipping between the sheets and taking me into his arms. He kissed my lips, my eyes, my breasts.

This is the way it will be, I thought. *I am his woman now.*

It did not disturb me that he should bed me on the night of Catherine's funeral. Death makes the need for life more vivid. But it is not the sort of thing I want the world to know.

Within that same year, 1759, I gave birth to Peter, our first son. From then on, I was busy mothering Nancy, Polly and John, as well as my own child. I continued to keep Sir William's books, and my duties increased as he gave into my charge his entire estate.

His duties as Superintendent of Indian Affairs carried him frequently from home, but he was with me often enough to beget seven more children over the next fifteen years.

Sir William was always famous for his hospitality. After he built Johnson Hall, a handsome house considerably larger than Fort Johnson, we were constantly entertaining guests, both Indian and white. There was always plenty to eat and drink. Our guests did as they pleased. Sir William and I normally retired before midnight, but we would hear the talking and laughing continue downstairs until three in the morning.

There was serious purpose behind all this hospitality, for revolution was brewing. In the Mohawk Valley there were many who wished to break away from Britain. Sir William's responsibility as Superintendent of Indian Affairs was to keep the Iroquois nations loyal, for if there should be war, England would need their help. I was of great assistance to my husband in this. It pleased my people to see that I was an equal partner in Sir William's life.

My husband foresaw the coming war, but did not live to witness it. In 1774 he died of a stroke suffered while delivering a speech to an Iroquois council. He left me two hundred pounds and a female slave.

John Johnson, Sir William's heir, took over the title and the estate. As was proper, he took up residence in Johnson Hall. I could have continued to live in the small dowager house nearby, but I was only thirty-eight and needed activity in my life. With Sir John's approval, I moved to Canajoharie with my children and opened a general store.

Canajoharie was where I expected to spend the rest of my life, but the outbreak of war changed my plans. With my children, I was driven from the Mohawk Valley, taking refuge first at Fort Niagara and then at Fort Haldimand on Carleton Island, near the place which later became Kingston. Along the way, I became a diplomat in my own right.

In the morning, just before the Mississaga docked in Kingston, I heard a tapping at my cabin door.

"Come in," I called, suspecting that my visitor was Mrs. Simcoe.

There she stood before me, arrayed in a long, grey travelling cloak, and wearing a bonnet lavishly trimmed with silk flowers. She closed the cabin door.

"I have come to bid you farewell," she said. "You must be happy to be home."

"Very happy. I have three daughters in Kingston, as well as a comfortable home. My house, as you may know, was the government's gift to me, along with my pension."

"From what I have heard, you earned a greater reward than anyone could pay. Governor Simcoe has told me that without your persuasion, the Iroquois nations would not have remained loyal to Britain. And you did more than that, he said. You supplied arms to Loyalists. You gathered information that led to the British victory at Oriskany."

"Yes, I did all that."

The silence that fell between us was broken by the sound of voices outside the cabin and loud thumping above us on the deck.

"I must join my husband and children. We must prepare to disembark." The Governor's Lady opened the door, and with a slight bow she said, "It was a pleasure to have made your acquaintance."

"The honour is mine."

I listened to her footsteps retreat along the passage until they were lost amid the general noise. My own packing was done. For a few minutes I had time to dwell on the memories locked in my heart.

I had indeed rendered service to England by carrying on my husband's work after he died. I had also raised eight children. And when the war ended and settlement of Upper Canada began, I had helped to obtain for the Six Nations the grant of the Haldimand Tract, six miles wide on both sides of the Grand River. That was my last achievement. I pray that my people will find prosperity there, and a lasting home.

Author's Notes

Contemporary Observations

September 13, 1795. On board the Mississaga. At 6 this morning we weighed anchor. The Ft & Newark [now Niagara-on-the-Lake] looked very pretty under a rising Sun as we left Niagara River. The wind is fair & we keep the South Shore so I hope to discern the entrance of the Genesee River. . . . Orders were given for my accommodation that no person should have a Passage to Kingston on the Mississaga, but I relented in favour of Brant's sister who was ill & very desirous to go. She speaks English well & and is a civil & very sensible old woman.

Mrs. Simcoe's Diary. (Ed. Mary Quayle Innis). Macmillan of Canada. 1965.

December 9, 1793. Capt. Brant dined here. . . . He wore an English Coat with a handsome Crimson Silk blanket lined with black & trimmed with gold fringe & wore a Fur Cap, round his neck he had a string of plaited sweet hay. It is a kind of grass which never loses its pleasant scent. The Indians are very fond of it. (Ibid.)

On June 4, 1793, General Benjamin Lincoln attended a ball given at Niagara by Lieutenant Governor Simcoe. Among other details of the ball, General Lincoln observed:

What excited the best feelings of my heart was the ease and affection with which the ladies met each other; although there were a number present whose mothers sprang from the aborigines of the country [These included the daughters of Sir William Johnson and Molly Brant.] They appeared as well dressed as the company in general, and intermixed with them in a manner which evinced at once the dignity of their own minds and the good sense of others. . . .

(Quoted by Mary Quayle Innis, p. 10)

Indian agent Daniel Claus commented in 1779, "One word from her goes farther with them (the Iroquois) than a thousand from any white man without exception who in general must purchase their interest at a high rate." Alexander Fraser, commanding Carleton Island in 1779-1780, declared that the Indians' "uncommon good behaviour is in a great measure ascribed to Miss Molly Brant's influence over them, which is far superior to that of all their Chiefs put together."

Molly Brant died at her home in Kingston on April 16, 1796, at the age of sixty. Her body was interred in the burial ground of St. George's Church, where St. Paul's Church is now located.

Joseph Brant was born in 1742 and died in 1807 at his home in the place that would become Burlington, Ontario. His house is now Joseph Brant Museum.

Sir William Johnson (1715-1774) emigrated from Ireland at the age of twenty-three in order to manage the land granted to his uncle, Admiral Sir Peter Warren. Knighted for his services in the French and Indian Wars (1755-1760), Johnson was a shrewd trader and businessman. His Indian name, Warragghivagey, means "He who does much business".

Sir William Johnson and Molly Brant had eight children who survived infancy, two sons and six daughters. They were educated in Montreal. One son died in battle and the other became a farmer. The daughters all married, most to non-aboriginals. Within a few generations, Molly's descendants were thoroughly anglicized.

WE SEE THEE RISE

Mary-Eileen McClear

In the first place, there was no cow. Well, there was a cow. We had a cow. But I was not about to take her on that walk, and besides, who would believe I was leading her away from the house and the barn to be milked?

No, no cow. I simply told the sentries I was going to St. David's to visit my brother, Charles, who was ill, and they let me pass. And I did go there, didn't I? Went to him in the hope that he would be well enough to take the news to FitzGibbon. But he wasn't. And Hannah's boys had up and joined the militia. Hard to believe they were old enough. That left me.

Forgive me. I should have introduced myself. I am Laura Ingersoll Secord. I am 93 years old. I am not a heroine. I am simply a woman who did what had to be done.

I can talk about the walk now. Not like in the early days. Well, we didn't dare talk about it then, did we? Not right after it happened. The Americans were still very much in the area. They would not have taken kindly to the news that I had alerted FitzGibbon to their plan of attack. They were furious and humiliated at being so royally routed – 500 Americans defeated by the Native forces and 50 British soldiers!

But I can tell you about it now, and I will tell you the truth: I didn't want to go. The moment we overheard the plans of the Americans, my husband James and I looked at each other and I had a sinking feeling in my stomach because I knew I would have to go. And I didn't want to. I had five young children and an invalid husband. But someone had to carry the news. If FitzGibbon's forces were ambushed, why it would have given the Americans control of the peninsula. And who else was there to go? Clearly not James. The only reason he was still at home was because his knee had been so badly smashed at the Battle for Queenston Heights that he was not deemed a threat by the Americans. All of the other men and boys, and even the walking wounded, had been marched off as prisoners when the Americans returned, months after the Battle. But James wasn't walking much, not then and not easily for the rest of his life. The only men left were either too old, too young, or infirm. I would have to go – at least as far as St. David's. And then ... ? I was afraid.

I had too much time to think about it perhaps. Not like when I went onto the battlefield at Queenston Heights to find James. There was no choice, no thinking about that. Any woman would have done the same. The battle took place practically in our backyard. When stray bullets began to hit the house I gathered up the children and we ran farther away, to our neighbour's. I watched from the window as wounded men began to come down from the battlefield, helping each other as they limped along. I looked for James. Finally when the battle was winding down and I could hear only occasional shots, like the last kernels of corn popping over the fire, I went out to question those who passed. "Do you know my man, James Secord? Have you seen James Secord?"

One man stopped. "James Secord? Aye, I know him. He's hit. I passed him lying up there on the battlefield." Well, there was no thought about it at all. I picked up my skirts and I ran to find him.

But this was different. We had all night to plan. I had time to think, imagine, worry. I couldn't sleep.

I was up with the birds before it was even light. I left the house by 4 a.m. I still remember that morning clearly. I looked in on the children as they slept. Little Appolonia had her doll tucked up close to her. I remember the dress I wore that day. It was brown with orange flowers. I had my bonnet of course, and shoes. The only shoes I had left after our house had been ransacked, twice, by the Americans was a pair of light kid slippers. They would have to do. I packed a basket with some jam and cake – Charles always said I had a light touch with sweets – and then set off.

Even at that hour the air was heavy and humid. It was going to be another beastly hot day. I reached St. David's before breakfast and discovered Charles was still sick and Hannah's older boys gone. It was up to me after all. If I could have gotten anyone at all to go in my place, believe that I would have. I had more than an inkling of what lay ahead.

Hannah's daughter Elizabeth, who was twenty, insisted on coming along. I had my doubts, knowing her delicate constitution, but it did seem that it would be safer with two of us, rather than just one. No, now, that's just not true. How could two travel more quickly and quietly than one? The truth was, I was glad of the company. I didn't want to face it alone.

And so we set out. There are no words that can make you fully understand what it was like. Heat, insects, pounding sun, pain, exhaustion. The fear of being followed and watched. Knowing that if you were caught it might well mean your death. My story would be that I was lost, but it was far-fetched at best. I might well have been suspected as a spy. And what would have become of the children then? Mary would have had to be a mother to the others and she only twelve. Appolonia was only two. She wouldn't even have remembered me. And James? No doubt the American soldiers would have punished him as well.

James had suggested that the route should not be a direct one to FitzGibbon, for that would lead straight through American forces. Rather it should go 16 kilometres to Shipman's Corners and from there down to DeCew House through British territory.

The road to Shipman's Corners was scarcely a road at all. In most places it was little more than a path, densely overgrown and leading through the swamp, which steamed in the heat. It was wet and slippery and smelled of dank decaying things. We heard slithering sounds, small splashes; even the birds sounded eerie and ominous. Mosquitoes swarmed us but after a while we couldn't spare the energy to swat at them; we were covered in welts from their bites. Invisible eyes seemed to be on all sides. Hour after hour. Poor Elizabeth tried so hard to keep a steady pace but I was constantly having to wait for her to catch up or to catch her breath.

Twelve hours. Twelve hours from the time I left home that morning we reached Shipman's Corners. The sight of that house – the homely scene of barnyard and garden – brought tears to my eyes and I would have given anything ...

I barely stopped, other than to explain to Mrs. Shipman what I was doing and leave an exhausted Elizabeth in her care. She gave me a cool cloth to wash my face and neck and sent me off with bread and meat and fresh water to drink. The day was passing too quickly. I had come sixteen kilometres, but I still had twelve to go. The most difficult and dangerous part of the trip was ahead of me and much of it up the steep escarpment.

I was afraid to go by the road, even though this was supposed to be British territory, so I followed Twelve Mile Creek. The route took me through brambles and berry patches. The willows along the creek were a godsend but every bush and shrub in the dense undergrowth seemed to be on the side of the Americans, determined to hold me back. My skin was burned, my feet blistered and bleeding.

People ask what I thought of during those last six hours when I walked alone. I tell them that much of the time I could only think of where to put my feet so that I wouldn't stumble or fall. I tell them I thought of the children and James and that I wondered if I would ever reach my destination.

But I do not tell them that I thought about the Americans: the American soldier who helped me bring James home after the Battle at Queenston Heights; the Americans who looted and pillaged our home and business twice – not just stealing (I suppose I can understand theft) but wantonly destroying what they did not take. Why did they do that? I do not tell them that I thought of the American officers who ordered me to cook for them but always brought enough food to ensure that plenty would be left over for James and the children and me. I do not tell them I thought of the American friends and relatives I had to leave behind on that other, even longer, trip made through dense wilderness when I was eighteen. I was with my father and stepmother and the others then, of course. I hadn't wanted to go on that trip either because it meant leaving behind all my friends, most of my relatives, and my home in Massachusetts.

It might surprise you to know that we were not Loyalists. James' parents were Loyalists and he himself arrived here when he was only three. But I am, was, an American, born and bred. My father's family had been in the American colonies for over 200 years. My father fought against the British in 1776 and was fiercely proud of the independence he helped to win, the nation he helped create. We all were. I was raised on stories of the heroes of that war – women among them. Molly Hays: they called her Molly Pitcher because she took water to the men on the battlefield and when her husband fell wounded, she fired his cannon. Margaret

Corbin helped defend Ft. Washington. And Betsy Ross. Now, mind you, she only sewed a flag. These were my heroes. But after the war, financial problems meant a move north where a land grant was available. And so we came, and I met James, and Upper Canada became my new home.

But I do not tell all of this, because if I do, then I will also tell that I wondered what it really mattered if the Americans took over the peninsula.

I was an American, I had lived as an American and been proud of it. I knew there were good and bad Americans, just as there were good and bad British. What did it really matter? I only wanted the fighting to be over.

That is what I thought of as I walked. Walked! I walked, I trod, I trudged, I slipped, tripped and picked my way. At times I even crawled. I balanced on slick fallen logs to cross the creek. You could practically wring the air it was so humid. And hot! I was drenched – from my bonnet down by sweat, from my hem up from the swamp, the beaver pools and the creeks. My dress was filthy, covered in mud and dirt and torn. I stank.

I watched for rattlesnakes, for bears near the berry patches, and wild pigs. As the evening wore on and night began to fall I watched and listened for wolves and wildcats. And always I was wary of any sound that might have been made by two feet, instead of four.

It seemed as if I had been walking all my life, and as if I would never stop. I just kept putting one foot in front of the other, keeping the setting sun on my right. Six more hours. It was deep twilight – virtually dark – and I began to despair of arriving in time, or even arriving at all. I struggled up over a hill, bent over and pulling myself up, and walked straight into an encampment of Native men. They knew something was coming – I must have sounded like a bear crashing my way through the brush – but I don't know which of us was more surprised. They shouted at me. I heard the word "woman" spoken over and over. I managed to stand and asked loudly for FitzGibbon. Eventually they led me to him and I told him that there was no time to lose. The Americans were planning an ambush in the next twenty-four hours. He made me say who I was, and asked again and again where I had come from and how I had arrived there. Then he called his ensigns. He bowed over my hand, filthy as it was, and he left.

So that was it. I had walked for eighteen hours, from 4 a.m. 'til after 10 at night. I was thirty-seven years old but I felt ... ancient. I could barely move. FitzGibbon's aide escorted me to a neighbouring farmhouse and I slept. By the time I awoke, the battle was over.

People ask how I could have made that journey. FitzGibbon said later he was amazed that such a delicate woman could have done it. Sometimes I ask myself where the strength came from and you know what the irony is? I think it was plain Yankee determination. That strength was born and bred in me in Massachusetts, fostered by the stories of the heroes of another war, and honed on our trek north to Upper Canada.

The better question to ask might be: Did I not feel any hesitation in betraying the troops of the country of my youth? The answer is not a simple one. There was no set of scales with my American background, friends and relatives, on one side, my life in Canada, wounded husband, and ransacked house on the other.

Just last year I had an insight. Last year: 1867. You see, I brought that Yankee determination with me and it blended with the strengths and skills I gained here, and ended up as something new. Last year it came to me that what I did was not necessarily for the British, nor against the Americans. It was for myself, my family, my neighbours, my community. It was for the homes we were carving out of a wilderness, for the lives we were making in a new place. It was for the right to live our lives without the fear of soldiers and battles in our backyards. It was for Canada. I just didn't know it then.

Well, I have told you what I did, as I remember it. I have seen my actions with the perfect vision of hindsight. If you'll excuse me, I'm tired. I'm sure they've turned down my bed for me. Now, if I could just have a bit of chocolate before I sleep.

Author's Note

Laura Secord (1775 - 1868) was a Canadian heroine of the War of 1812. She became aware of an American plan to launch a surprise attack on the troops of British Lieutenant James FitzGibbon. If successful, the Americans would have gained control of the Niagara Peninsula. Secord walked for eighteen hours, through 32 kilometres of wilderness, to warn FitzGibbon. As a result of the information she brought, the small force of British troops, along with a larger force of Native allies, was able to ambush, defeat, and take prisoner the much larger American contingent in the Battle of Beaverdams (June 24, 1813).

I was asked to tell a story about Laura Secord for the annual Storytellers of Canada / Conteurs du Canada conference in 2007. My first response was to say no, because I thought her story was too well known and I wanted to tell about someone who would be more interesting to listeners. I agreed to tell, instead, about Dr. Elizabeth Bagshaw, one of the first female doctors in Canada and head of Canada's first birth control clinic. No sooner had I hung up the phone, however, then a voice came into my head, as clear as a bell, and said, "In the first place, there was no cow."

"Laura?" I said aloud. "Is that you?"

I phoned the conference organizers back and said I had changed my mind. I would tell Laura's story after all. And I did. Laura spoke to me only once more after that. It was when I had thought the story was done and was about to test it on a group of listeners. She announced, "I didn't want to do it, you know." So, it was back to the computer. Discovering what might have been going through her mind was a fascinating journey of research and imagination. I only wish Laura would come back one more time to tell me if I got it right.

MAIDEN AUNT

Richard Van Holst

Miss Georgina Hogarth is walking at a rather quick pace toward Harley Street. She is just over thirty, although the passers-by, should they take the time to look, might guess her to be considerably younger. She is of medium height, somewhat round of face, and neither very slender nor extremely stout. Her hair is a quite ordinary brown enlivened by red highlights, but these are hidden by her bonnet. Her dress is not without fashion. But it is Georgina's eyes that attract notice; they are blue, and quite piercing when she is in a certain mood. These eyes are presently frowning, but whether in irritation or worry it is hard to say. Her walking companion, an older, plumper, motherly looking woman, does not see the expression in Georgina's eyes, because it is all she can do to keep up with her. But Georgina herself is not paying much attention to her surroundings, for she is in no danger of getting lost. She knows the streets of London well, having trod them extensively with her brother-in-law Charles.

In fact, until not too long ago, those highly enjoyable jaunts were a treasured part of her life. Charles, bursting with nervous energy after several hours of work, would feel the overwhelming compulsion to walk, almost at a canter, through the streets. Sometimes a hapless guest, lured by the thought of seeing the shop where Little Nell had lodged, or the tavern in which Bill Sikes and Nancy had beguiled an evening, had to struggle to keep up with him. If there were no such gullible guest staying at the house, however, and if her sister Catherine and the children were suitably occupied, Georgina would put on her traveling suit and go with him. Catherine gave the impression she felt sorry that Georgina must face this challenge, yet grateful to be spared it herself. Catherine, in fact, had never been truly quick on her feet and had been made plump and yet more indolent by many pregnancies. But not Georgina. Having lived in the Dickens household since she was fifteen, she had early trained her feet to match Charles' martial pace, the better to hear the comments that cascaded from him as he sped along.

Most of the people in the neighbourhood knew the two of them by sight and she received almost as many friendly greetings as he. Only once, in fact, had her identity been mistaken. It was a little incident which hadn't seemed to mean much at the time; now that she looked back on it, however, the whole affair seemed rather prophetic. Georgina had been deep in conversation with Charles, when suddenly a man with a double chin, large, brilliant teeth, sharp eyes and an oily manner had swooped down upon them. Thomas Mitton, Charles' one time friend and solicitor, with his niece in tow, was suddenly looming before them, greeting Charles as if they had just met at the club. He'd nodded familiarly to Georgina and made small talk, while the niece, a pale sandy-haired girl of about seventeen had hung back timorously. Finally she had tugged gently at the solicitor's sleeve. "Please, Uncle Thomas," she had said, "will you not present me to Mr. and Mrs. Dickens?"

"Oh no, Penelope! You're a little mistaken there," her uncle had said, with a cheerful laugh. "This is not Mrs. Dickens; it is Miss Hogarth, the *sister* of Mrs. Dickens. She is quite an accomplished actress and musician if I remember rightly!"

Miss Mitton had kept her lips politely pursed, but it was clear from her expression that she wondered why a young gentleman should be out strolling with his sister-in-law rather than with his wife. Charles had adroitly mentioned that Catherine had just come through another confinement and that, since she was resting comfortably and the children were being looked after, he had invited Georgina to take the air with him. This had provoked a burst of hilarity from Mitton.

"Well done, sir! And what famous personage did you name your offspring after this time? No doubt you've called it Benjamin Disraeli Dickens? Or Augustus Egg Dickens?" (Here he had actually winked at Georgina!) "Perhaps Nicholas Nickleby Dickens? Or Little Nell Dickens?"

At the mention of this last name, Miss Mitton was unable to resist telling Charles how inexpressibly sad she had been to hear of the death of Little Nell. Charles had softened at that, having himself suffered intense pangs of regret over her death, though the instruments of execution had been his own pen and paper. And after some inconsequential chatter Mitton had hooked his niece's hand around a pointed elbow, and with a rather peremptory, "Come along, Penny," had swooped away.

When he had been sure that the interlopers were out of earshot, Charles had given Georgina a look that was at once merry and rueful. "I know you don't much care for Thomas, but he was a good friend to me in my younger days. And he has performed some useful services for me."

"Well, I have never met anyone who reminded me so much of Uriah Heep. I do believe he teased me about acting in some of your plays. And I am sure that his mention of Mr. Egg was a further bit of slyness!"

"You may be right. I might have let some comment slip shortly after your portrait was finished." Suddenly, a tremor passed through his entire body. Twisting his lips into a crooked smirk, buckling his knees to an alarming degree and thrusting his chin out at an oblique angle, he had pulled his hat off with one hand and offered her the other as if it were a dead fish. Ducking his head, he had peered at her from heavily lidded eyes. "Beggin' yer most gracious pardon most 'umbly, Oi'm sure, Miss 'Ogawrth. Oi on'y wants ter be of service to yer in me own 'umble ker-passity. 'Cos, as yew well knows, Miss 'Ogawrth, Oi'm a very 'umble person, Oi am. Most 'umble indeed, Miss, Oi do assure yer!"

"Ugh! Unhand me, you *odious* creature!" she had squealed in mock revulsion. "You *Heep* of infamy!"

He had positively roared with laughter, as with a jerk of his spine, he had become his natural self again. He could metamorphose so completely into one of his own literary children that the passers-by would eye him with surprise.

Mitton's comments had some truth to them, however, for Georgina was not averse to treading the boards, in an amateur sort of way. Charles, with his extraordinary attention to detail, had organized some plays that had been quite well received and she had even performed with him for Her Majesty, accompanied by the Prince Consort and a small party. Prince Albert's laughter had caused Charles to twinkle brightly, in the way only he could. Though he had continued his antics, pretending to be unaware of his royal audience, his gratification was obvious to Georgina.

The theatre was in Charles' blood; he admitted as much himself, and said it had always been so. There was a quality about his large, dark eyes that attracted one's own eyes to him. His voice with its slight burr, by turns jolly or sad, but always intense, commanded attention. She herself had fallen under his spell when she was very young.

From the age of eight, she had been fascinated by the bright clothes, the luminous eyes that seemed to see everything, the easy laugh. She had never forgotten the day when, dressed in a rented sailor's uniform, he had jumped through the drawing room window of her parents' home, danced a hornpipe and walked out, whistling loudly and twirling his moustaches. The family had stared at each other: her mother not knowing whether to be offended or frightened, Catherine tranquilly amused, Mary gazing with sparkling eyes at the window through which he had just vanished like a djinn, Georgina herself barely able to suppress the urge to get up and dance. A few minutes later Charles, in his regular clothes and every whisker in place, had strolled back in through the door as if nothing had happened and, with a courtly bow, gravely offered the usual courtesies. As he had intended, Catherine had been suitably impressed and he had made a stir in the family.

This incident, in fact, had made such a stir, that Georgina had often used it as a bed-time story for the children. Charles would have told it much better, of course, but even so, her version had been a favourite with them. She could still remember most of it:

The King and Queen of Scotland and their children (all with names curiously similar to those of the Hogarth family) *deciding that their castle in Scotland is too small, betake themselves on an epic ramble, and, after various rustic adventures, arrive somewhat footsore in London, where, dodging pickpockets and scoundrels of all kinds, they soon find a more commodious dwelling. They have an accidental but memorable meeting with a young prince disguised as a sailor* (wearing, of course, a bright orange waistcoat just like Charles'). *The exotically garbed Prince Bozzini* (rather than vanishing as Charles had done) *throws himself on his knees before the fair Princess Catherina, who, naturally, is nearly swooning with delight. "O Princess Catherina," he declaims with evident enjoyment, "I have only a small part of London as my kingdom, and my palace isn't as large as yours, but if you marry me, I shall love you as long as the sun endures, and I shall do all in my power to make you happy." The Princess asks her Queen-Mamma "Do you think I should?" The Queen-Mamma answers, "Ask your heart, and do what it tells you." So Princess Catherina inquires very solemnly, "Heart of mine, do you think I should? Thump once for yes and twice for no." Her heart thumps very loudly, once for yes. And in a trice they are married.*

"What about the sisters, the Princesses Marianna and Georgianna?" one of the children would invariably ask. "Did *they* ever marry?" Georgina had not wanted to tell the children, even in fictional guise, how the frail Mary, ashen-faced and panting, had lain curled like a wounded animal on her bed the night before her death. How the embers of her life had gone out in Charles' arms the next day. How Charles' grief had erupted. How Catherine, for once efficient and practical, had gone about the household business with silent, white-lipped grief – and had suffered her first miscarriage a few weeks later. So Georgina had invented a soothingly melodramatic speech for the Princess Marianna to utter in low melodic tones before gliding serenely into the next life. As for the Princess Georgianna, she had become a pirate on the South Seas, having numerous adventures with Bozzini's heroic progeny and slaying any would-be suitor that came within reach of her cutlass.

In reality, Georgina had not treated her suitors with quite so much belligerence. Poor little Augustus Egg, so painfully taciturn in her presence, had fallen in love with her as he had completed her portrait, and she'd had a hunch that both Charles and Catherine had encouraged him. Because he was Charles' friend, she had discouraged the soft-spoken young bachelor as gently as possible. She had, already, become far too comfortable with Charles and Catherine. And there were the children to take care of after all. To them she was "Auntie Georgy" and it was becoming more and more difficult even to think of parting from them. She had once told Charles in a burst of disdain that she was not "in *l'oeuf* with *l'Oeuf*." No, she could no more see herself as "Madame de Poultrie" than as any of those other things Mitton had teased her about.

"Accomplished actress indeed!"

"I beg your pardon, Miss Georgina?" asks Anne Brown.

Georgina realizes with a start that she has spoken this remark aloud. "It's nothing, Anne," she says. I was just thinking about ... about all the trouble that has come upon the family."

Anne Brown nods sympathetically and continues to plod, puffing, after Georgina, who marches purposefully on with a scowl. It is actually not nothing, she thinks to herself. It could be everything. Her lively bustling life with Charles and Catherine could be gone, her bond with the children severed, her summer jaunts through Europe ended. Her position in the house would be closed to her if she herself were accused of – but she could not even bring herself to think about what she was accused of. And if she were forbidden his house, then her reputation in society – and with it all chance of getting a husband, or even a post as governess – would be ruined. She would be once again closely confined to a rather small house with her querulous mother who had started the rumours in the first place. Well, perhaps her mother had not started them herself, but she had done nothing to prevent their being spread, and thereby lent them credence.

And all because of a round-faced chit of a girl with golden tresses and large soulful eyes, (who was not even a very accomplished actress, come to think of it), that Nelly person from the Haymarket theatre. If only he had never seen her, never started mooning over her, never started comparing her to the placid Catherine or to his ethereal memory of Mary, never tried to help her and her family. And if only he hadn't sent her that confounded brooch! The impulse was innocent enough in itself – on the surface of things anyway. But that dolt of a jeweler, assuming that Charles was sending a present to his wife, had not bothered to look at the directions on the packet. And so that wretched little bauble, engraved with his initials C.J.H.D. and bearing the portrait of one of the most recognizable faces in England, had come to Catherine's notice!

Catherine, as Georgina could have predicted, had not reacted well. In the face of her anger and aggrieved tears, Charles had mustered all his powers of persuasion. Was it necessary to separate? Could they not make arrangements? Would she not be satisfied with her own apartment in the house? Could she not bring herself to appear, for form's sake alone, at the dinner-parties his friends expected from him? To all of which Catherine had opposed red eyes and a tightly closed mouth. Next he had tried firmness. He had often sent gifts and mementos to those who had worked under his direction. Catherine knew that! – everyone knew that! That "creature", as Catherine had called her, was totally innocent. In fact Catherine should go to visit her and see for herself – and apologize! The red eyes had only grown larger and the mouth had closed even more tightly. Then, hoping that her sister might make her see reason, he had begged Georgina to try what she could. But even to her Catherine had said only, "Georgina, my dear, I have suffered for years. I cannot bear any more of this."

Catherine had poured forth her grievances to her mother in an impassioned letter. Mrs. Hogarth, whom Charles had long viewed with an unfriendly eye, had proposed a visit. In itself this would have been dire enough, but there was more: her mother had threatened to sue Charles in the Divorce Courts.

So Charles had retreated, but not in defeat. Not yet. Rivers of letters had begun to flow from the house to his friends and his solicitor, seeking information about the new marriage laws. Had the law changed since the short-lived and unsuccessful bill of 1854? What about the new Matrimonial Causes Act, the one that had been passed last year? Would that help or hinder his case if his mother-in-law were to make good her threat to attack him?

As far as Georgina was concerned, she could cheerfully have thrown all this correspondence, as well as that accursed trinket and Miss Nelly, into the mouth of Vesuvius.

But if the truth be told, it had begun long before Nelly. Vesuvius was the place where she had first noticed that there was a smouldering thing creating fissures between Charles and Catherine. Georgina could still see Salvatore, the head guide, turning to explain in a mixture of explosive Neapolitan and broken but unctuous English, underscored by extravagantly fluttering hands, how the party would proceed. Then he had interrupted himself to expostulate with an underling: "*Marònna! Nun me scuccià, gnurante!*" He had turned to explain to Charles. "Pliss esscuse, Signore. Dissa boya, 'e don' know 'ow to put da saddal to da 'orse." Catherine had furrowed her brows as Charles winked to reassure her that these men could not be all that incompetent. The horses, made skittish by the presence of tourists, snorted and shied at the shouts of the guides, as if, through some sort of magnetic influence, the volcano itself were transmitting to them its own unease. Then, finally the motley procession, with the volatile Salvatore at its head, had wound its way cautiously up the slope, picking a precarious path among piles of jumbled rocks. A staccato cough had risen from the whole party as they'd gagged on the sulphurous fumes emitted here and there from seething fissures, the Mountain rumbling like a belching demon, surfeited on a diet of the hapless damned. Catherine had barely suppressed a scream as the litters were jolted and tipped by the profusely sweating bearers.

"*Stateve accùorto, fesse!*" Salvatore had barked. "*Nun facite cadé 'e ffemmene 'ngrese!*"

Georgina had looked at Catherine inquiringly. *Are you all right?* Her answering smile, wan but brave, had said: *I weathered a sea-voyage to America; I will survive this!*

The sun had set like a glowing coal over the Mountain, the sudden darkness only slightly dissipated by the party's smoking torches. The moon, livid and distant, had transmogrified the terrain into a landscape of black punctuated by deeper black. Suddenly there had been a halt. Catherine had inquired fretfully for Charles. He had come to her, but his mind was clearly elsewhere; he remained determined to scale the central cone even though Catherine had implored him not to. He'd had no time for such nonsense and gripping his staff, moved away with the guide. Creeping off, they had been almost instantly obscured by vapour. Georgina, fascinated, had squinted into the distance, trying to mark their passage. Suddenly a shout. Charles had reached the top and was peering into the cone. After a moment he'd drawn back a little, and brimming with high spirits, had begun to caper.

"*Azzo!*" one of the guides had gasped, crossing himself. "*'O 'ngrese è tuccato 'e capa!*"

Another, shaking his head, had replied, "*'O Signore Stravagante sta pe' cadé dint'o pertuso da Muntagna!*"

"*E comme no?*" a third had agreed. "*Chella, 'a Muntagna so magnarrà!*"

"What is happening? What are they saying?" Catherine had asked.

Out of consideration for her sister's feelings, Georgina had omitted the general assessment of the state of Charles' reason and answered, "They are afraid Charles will be devoured by the mountain."

Catherine's hand had fluttered to her mouth. "Heavens! If he is not careful he may fall in!" But before long, he was heading back to them. Picking his way over the slippery ground with methodical deliberation, testing footholds and casting his dark glinting eyes here and there, he resembled nothing so much as his pet raven, Grip, stalking through the garden in search of shiny trinkets.

Beside them once again, he had said something melodramatic about nature in all her tragic grandeur, about the immortal Dante and the sufferings of the souls in torment. He had reached to embrace Catherine but she had recoiled in horror. "Charles! You are on fire!" she had screamed, and Georgina, fearing that her sister would actually faint, had rummaged in her reticule for the bottle of smelling salts she always carried for just such emergencies. For his hair and clothes had actually been smouldering. The guides had mobbed him, striking at him repeatedly to smother the flames that were trying to kindle. "Once again, as you see," he'd said, winking at Georgina, "I am blazing away!" This was the phrase Charles always used when the writing was coming easily and he had just spent a morning pouring forth a stream of prose. Georgina had chuckled in spite of herself and received a reproachful glance from Catherine. "Mousie," he'd murmured soothingly to Catherine, "please do not fret. All will be well." Georgina knew that this endearment, first employed by Charles during their courtship, was one that Catherine had come finally to detest – she had in fact been about to retort sharply but, thinking better of it, merely said, "Such a fine hat! And now it is ruined!" He had returned her frown, and the journey down the mountain had begun. It had not been without its perils. The travelers had to form a chain to ensure that no one lost his footing; in spite of this precaution, one of the other tourists, a plump Englishman, had actually toppled into a crevice! Luckily the guides, shouting and scrambling, had managed to haul him out with little more than bruises.

Georgina, suddenly struck by a thought, almost laughs. Years from now they will tell their grandchildren tall tales about the mad Englishman who nearly threw himself into the mouth of the Mountain. But a more serious memory intrudes to spoil her merriment, the memory of the day the storm broke over her own head.

She had actually heard Charles yell from his writing room. Anne Brown had gone to see what the matter was, and had come to fetch her, breathless and red-faced. "The master wants to see you, Miss Georgina, and he ain't over happy." With foreboding she had walked into the room where he had been writing. Uncharacteristically, papers were scattered on the floor. "Look at this!" he had shouted. "Just look!" His face was mottled, and he was spitting and stuttering with rage. He had flapped the newspaper at her indignantly. "*Look! Look at it!*"

She had read the following:

> "Long ago, when the illustrious Mr. D*** burst upon the literary horizon like an exuberant sun, he gave us a number of portraits of society which both amused his readers and instructed them as to the foibles of the middle classes. In a sketch entitled 'The Four Sisters' he describes four chaste maidens of the name of Willis, who, being acquainted with one Mr. Robinson, decide that they will enter into more commodious and convenient living arrangements with him. The behaviour of three of the sisters at the marriage of the fourth and youngest leaves the neighbourhood in doubt of which of the Miss Willises has actually entered into the matrimonial state. This mystery is solved only by the birth of an infant. According to the rumours circulating at present in the City of London (and this writer has no desire either to besmirch the reputation of the author in question, or to affirm or deny the rumours herein alluded to), Mr. D*** has taken a page from his own jejune jottings. For hearsay would have it that he has been enamoured of three of the fair daughters of the house of H***, one of whom is lamentably deceased, the other two being at present members of his own domestic circle. In other words, there are those who wonder whether his sister-in-law, Miss H*** the younger, could have a closer relationship to his children than that of a beloved aunt. One wonders indeed which of his literary creations he will come to resemble most: Stephen Blackpool or Josiah Bounderby ..."

With a gasp, she had sat down rather hard.

And so, to protect himself and Georgina from accusations of immoral conduct, to safeguard his reputation, to keep up the facade of a tranquil domestic existence, which he felt was fast crumbling around him, Charles had devised the scheme that she should go to the surgery on Harley Street. If she were nervous of being seen, she could go by a circuitous route, early in the morning. He would pay for a hansom cab if she wished privacy on her journey. Or she could walk – she knew the streets as well as he. Anne Brown had danced attendance on her mistress long enough, and he was sure Catherine could be persuaded to do without her for one afternoon. (Georgina could simply say that she needed the maid's help on an errand – it was needless to burden Catherine with further particulars.) Moreover, Anne's presence might be soothing. He had no misgivings as to the outcome, of course; in fact her undoubted virginity would serve to make his case unassailable. He knew Georgina's conduct to be exemplary in all things. She was not a mother to his children in fact (whatever the papers insinuated), but she was little short of it in the affection she had always borne them. Even Catherine could not say less – no matter what her mercenary mother persuaded her to believe. Mrs. Hogarth's motives must be terribly unnatural if she could sacrifice Georgina's reputation to ensure financial security and social acceptance for Catherine! Was not his mother-in-law's real motive the desire to punish him? And had he not offered Catherine a decent settlement so that they could avoid the shame and the expense of a public divorce? But he was straying from the matter at hand. He would write to Dr. Elliotson, his own family physician, at once to ask him to take the case. If Elliotson could not do it himself, as he was often very busy, he would be sure to recommend someone who could be trusted.

"Well, Miss Georgina," says Anne Brown, puffing. "This is Harley Street. At last. And there is. The surgery. Exactly where Mr. Dickens. Said it. Would be."

"So it is, Anne," she says.

"Don't distress yourself, Miss Georgina – I'm sure you've nothing to worry about."

"I hope not indeed, Anne." She pauses so that her companion can catch her breath.

After a moment Anne Brown continues, eager to offer encouragement. "It's nothing like what happened to Mr. Dickens the year Master Walter was born, you know, Miss. O' course that was afore you came to us, I s'pose. You'll have the tiniest bit o' discomfort, perraps, but nothing like what the master had!"

It was true that Anne had come to the family even before Georgina herself. She had been Catherine's maid a long time, since before her marriage to the rarely glimpsed Mr. Cornelius. In fact, Charles was so used to addressing her by her maiden name of Brown that he sometimes seemed to forget that she had a life outside the family. And, in deference to this idiosyncrasy, dutifully imitated by the rest of the household, the loyal domestic had never bothered to correct him.

And now, although Anne means well, Georgina wishes she had not chosen this particular moment to bring up Charles' fistula operation. It evokes the recollection of secretive perusals of her sister's letters, snatched during moments when her mother was not by, and carefully replaced in the escritoire. The young Georgina had vibrated between shock, fascination and compassion at Catherine's descriptions of the exquisite torture Charles had endured, both from the operation itself, and from the pain and boredom of his long convalescence.

Pressing her lips together stoically and gathering up her skirts, she climbs the steps. As Anne opens the door for her, she is greeted by a smell of coal smoke and sweat. No sooner is she in the door than she freezes. Behind her she can hear Anne's sharp intake of breath. For from the back room comes a sound which is not a scream, nor a retch, nor a gasp, but a mixture of all three. Then a man's voice exclaims with relief. A loud sobbing ensues, as of a child in deep distress.

A matronly looking woman seated at a square table with a large book before her, in which she has been recording names and figures, rises to greet her. This must be the physician's wife. Georgina gives her name to the woman, whose eyebrow rises immediately, and whose face is suffused with a look of compassion. "Ah," she says, "my husband said you would be coming, Miss Hogarth. He received a letter from Dr. Elliotson (who was his mentor at the University, you know) describing your, er, delicate situation." Worried that she has embarrassed Georgina, she continues to speak quickly. "He is engaged with a patient at present, Miss Hogarth. A little boy who was a-choking on a fish-bone, poor dear! But don't worry – it sounds as if my husband got it out at last. He should not be too long. Pray be seated." Georgina complies, and Anne Brown sits next to her, plumping down on the chair with a grateful sigh. On the far wall is a portrait, rather well done, of Her Majesty. The face is sedate and serious, graver than the face she remembers from the royal visit to the theatre. She gets a surprise next, for underneath the portrait of the Queen is one, smaller to be sure, of Dr. Elliotson, Charles' own physician. The large brown eyes stare back at her from the portrait, and except that the beard is perhaps fuller, he bears quite a resemblance to Charles. Close by, there are a few bookshelves. *Gray's Anatomy* has a place of eminence, like a father seated in dignity at the head of the table. But she then notices some of Dr. Elliotson's own works: *Principles and Practice of Medicine*, and *Numerous Cases of Surgical Operations without Pain in the Mesmeric State.*

Just as she is becoming interested in the titles, the door of the back room opens and a youngish woman, red-eyed and pale with relief, emerges, carrying a little boy, not more than two years old, who is clasping her tightly around the neck. He is in tears, and at once Georgina is filled with pity, thinking of her youngest nephew, Edward. The doctor follows and pats the boy on the head awkwardly but kindly. In a low voice he gives some advice to the nursemaid about giving the boy soft food for a while. "Well, well," he says, half to himself, after they have left, "there goes a young gentleman who will never truly enjoy fish." Then, turning briskly to his wife, he says, "I take it this lady is here for a consultation?"

"This is the, er, case Dr. Elliotson wrote to you about, my dear," explains his wife. "This is Miss Hogarth. She is a relation of Mr. Dickens."

Georgina curtsies. She hopes he does not mind, but she brought a companion along to assist her if necessary. The doctor, clearing his throat a little, says that is quite all right; some of his female patients bring companions. He ushers them into the examination room. Lingering a moment by the door, Georgina looks around, distracted from her nervousness by her curiosity. Close to the door, there is a small oak cabinet in which, ranged neatly on several shelves, she can see instruments laid in rows, their metal points glinting: the tiny sharp teeth of a bone saw grin at her from beside a tonsil guillotine. On a small table next to the cabinet lies an elongated ceramic dish containing the bits of fish bone that caused the doctor's previous client such discomfort, as well as the forceps used to extract them. On a second table sits the physician's leather satchel, its cavernous mouth open as if in pain. More instruments can be seen glimmering feebly from its depths. If Charles were here, he would no doubt imagine that Miss Jane Murdstone, having come to the surgery to have some of her metallic surfaces polished, has accidentally left her monstrous bag behind, and now, pining after its evil mistress, swollen with old age and indigestion, the bag is gasping in its vain efforts to vomit out Clara Copperfield's household keys at last. Georgina shudders involuntarily, and tries to hide the tremor by turning it into a discreet little shrug. She tells herself that such fancies are ridiculous – firmness is what is wanted! – and sits down on the chair proffered by the doctor's wife.

The doctor begins to explain to Georgina what will take place and points out to her the examination chair waiting quietly in the back corner by the window. It is a large chair, quite broad and high. Brightly polished nail studs twinkle like buttons at regular intervals along its arms and front. At the top, there is a little square headrest which seems disproportionate to the rest, as if, in an effort to make itself presentable to the female visitors it had hastily donned a hat that was too small for it. However, these weak attempts at finery are spoiled by the tripod whose extremities jut monstrously from underneath, like a set of gnarled goblin toes which have defied all attempts to cram them into respectable shoes.

The doctor goes to the cabinet and retrieves a small black, varnished tube, rather like a distended thumb, and begins a short discourse on Ferguson's speculum. His wife, familiar with this kind of speech, excuses herself and goes out. The doctor, relishing the chance to display his expertise, barely notices. But after a minute or two, he does see that the elegant lady has that strained expression of politeness one wears when one does not wish to offend – and her companion is looking positively bewildered. So, a little reluctantly, he breaks off his lecture and simply asks Georgina if there is any particular question she wishes to ask him.

Georgina answers – much to the surprise of the doctor's wife, whose curiosity has drawn her to listen at the keyhole – that she is highly conscious of the fact that his time is valuable, but that there is indeed something that is troubling her. Hesitantly, stumbling over her words, Georgina begins to relate an episode of her history that she has never confided to anyone. Once, about three years after she had moved into the Dickens household, she had gone horseback riding with a cousin of hers, a dashing young spark visiting from Edinburgh. She had decided to be adventurous and sit astride the horse's back, rather than riding sidesaddle as elegant young ladies are expected to do. Her cousin, far from discouraging her, had laughed uproariously and had even assisted her in mounting the animal.

But this is all the doctor's wife is to hear, for at that moment another client enters the surgery to claim her attention; it is a woman with a nervous complaint who often comes for a consultation. "Good day to you, Miss Mitton," says the doctor's wife. "My husband is engaged with a client at present. He may be occupied some little time. Pray be seated."

The doctor, surprisingly considerate, has listened patiently to Georgina's story, and explained that riding in that fashion for a brief period, if done once only, with reasonable care and without undue vigour, need not have obliterated completely the evidence of virtue. He has left

Anne Brown alone with her while she undressed. Now the doctor's wife returns once more, to help her into the chair and to adjust the position of her heels in the stirrups. The good lady explains what she is about to do before leaning over to crank the chair into a flat position; nevertheless, despite the warning, Georgina feels the same twinge of alarm she had experienced so many years before when she had climbed into the litter at the foot of Vesuvius. She remembers the apprehension in Catherine's face, but had somehow forgotten until this precise moment that she had shared the same fear. Anne Brown, standing behind the headrest looks into her face with mute sympathy. The doctor's wife helps her to shift herself into position, encouraging her all the while in the tone one uses with a fretful child. Georgina, who has often had to use this tone with Charles' children, rather resents being subjected to it herself. All the same, she musters a smile she hopes is brave and assures the other women that she is quite ready.

The pressure of her heels against the unpadded stirrups is uncomfortable. Her knees, bent and out to the side, stretch her legs in a way she does not like. The doctor's wife has placed a sheet over her, but she has the horrid sense that her body is laid bare for all to see. The doctor comes in and speaks to her, his tone calm. She begins to breathe more rapidly even before he lifts the sheet; when he does, there is a rush of air that unsettles her further. She sees him reach toward her, and tenses up. He assures her that he will use the utmost gentleness. She feels his index finger, and squeezes her eyes closed; his other hand is on her lower abdomen. After a moment, he withdraws his hand and she opens her eyes. She fixes her gaze on the ceiling, on one spot where the paint is starting to peel. At least there is no pain. Not yet.

She has always been healthy and so has not had much personal experience of pain. Which does not mean she is not intimately acquainted with it, thanks to the family. There was Charles' operation, as Anne Brown reminded her earlier. And Mary too. Catherine's seemingly unending pregnancies. And the miscarriages. Lying in this hard leather chair, in this unnatural position, with fear washing over her, she thinks that she now understands a little better the visceral terror of the childbed. Catherine had told her that one cannot truly understand unless one has actually gone through it. And she had always dismissed this statement as one more symptom of the despondency Catherine wore like a cloak during her perpetual confinements. Now, Georgina decides, in a wave of uncharacteristic remorse, that she has been entirely too hard on her poor sister. And so, for that matter, has Charles.

Though the doctor heated the speculum in warm water a few minutes ago, it is nevertheless cool when it touches her. She gasps and tenses. Her chest feels as if there is a weight on it. Her breaths come quick and shallow. Her pulse begins to race. She can feel the instrument advance slightly and rotate. The blades move, and the discomfort peaks into needle sharpness. Her upper teeth dig into her lower lip. She squeezes her eyes shut again. Her abdomen tightens. She wants to pull her heels out of the stirrups. But she must be still. She must stay calm.

After what seems like an hour but is really only a minute or two, the doctor rises from his crouched position. "It is my considered opinion, Miss Hogarth," he announces gravely, "that the scurrilous rumours presently circulating about you have no basis in fact." She expels a loud breath, and though she is still supine on the table, seems to sag. And here is Anne Brown, murmuring encouragement. The doctor's wife reappears, and, having swiftly eased her feet out of the stirrups, moves to crank the chair back into a seated position. She stretches her mouth into a smile and manages a few words of thanks. The doctor and his wife retire to let her dress, and no sooner has the door closed behind them than she is clinging to Anne and weeping with relief, her sobs ragged and ungraceful.

Miss Mitton, who has been waiting all this time in the outer room, is startled at the sound. But when Georgina finally emerges a few minutes later she gapes in open amazement and, without even waiting for the doctor's wife to introduce them, rises hastily and begins to speak with a spasmodic effusiveness. She remembers their first meeting with delight, as if they had shared a pleasant excursion, and inquires whether Mr. and Mrs. Dickens and all the children are well. Then, with a look of cloying solicitude, she hopes that Georgina is not suffering from a serious complaint. Georgina assures her that she is indeed in excellent health – and is spared the ordeal of further inquiries, for the doctor's wife now steps in and ushers Miss Mitton into the examination room.

Georgina, much to Anne Brown's relief, has allowed the doctor to summon a hansom cab for her. Though her eyes are still a little red, her face has resumed its habitual expression of determination. She has already begun to think about how she will tell him the good news and how happy he will be. She is looking forward to that.

She has always admired Charles. She has walked the streets of London with him many times. She has acted on the stage under his direction – not an easy thing, that! She has written his letters for him – and that is not easy either, for he often changes his mind about what he wants to say! She has been a companion to Catherine, as much for Charles' sake as for Catherine's. She has watched over their children with an almost maternal devotion. She has declined the proposals of more than one suitor, and has cheerfully resigned herself to a life that, so far, has had enough excitement to compensate for the loss of conjugal joys. But, even though her own family has sent her, as it were, up the cone of Vesuvius and forced her to stare into its very mouth as Charles once did, she has come back wiser. She knows what she has to do now. She must sit down with Charles and have a long talk with him. She must make him see reason! She must show him that Catherine, having endured so many trials for his sake, is deserving of the compassion and kindness due a devoted wife.

The hansom cab arrives, and Anne Brown goes out to open the door for her. The doctor is about to bid her a polite farewell when his wife, opening the door of the examination room, clears her throat and, having caught his eye, gives him a barely perceptible little frown. He turns back to Georgina with a grave expression. "Excuse me, Miss Hogarth," he says. "I do not wish to seem at all indelicate, but before you go, there *is* the small matter of, er, my fee."

She looks at him for a moment. Her lips twitch quizzically, on the verge of a smile. She says, "I am sure Mr. Dickens may be depended upon to satisfy you in that regard."

Translation of Napoletano phrases used in the story

NAPOLETANO: Marònna! Nun me scuccià, gnurante!

ENGLISH: By Our Lady! Don't bother me, stupid!

NAP: Stateve accùorto, fesse! ... Nun facite cadé 'e ffemmene 'ngrese!

ENG: Pay attention, you idiots! ... Don't let the English ladies fall!

NAP: 'Azzo!

ENG: Literal translation is difficult but this word expresses extreme astonishment.

NAP: 'O 'ngrese è tuccato 'e capa!

ENG: The Englishman is completely mad!

NAP: 'O Signore Stravagante sta pe' cadé dint'o pertuso da Muntagna!

ENG: Mister Oddball is going to fall into the hole in the Mountain! ("The Mountain" is the familiar designation given by the locals to Vesuvius.)

NAP: E comme no? ... Chella, 'a Muntagna so magnarrà!

ENG: But of course, [...] The Mountain will eat him.

Author's Note

I was still in elementary school when I began to stuff myself full of Dickens' works. As soon as Mr. Pickwick burst sun-like upon London in the opening chapter of The Pickwick Papers I was hooked on the author's style and on his sometimes gruesomely comic, but always memorable characters. And I have continued to enjoy his writing throughout my life.

But I never really understood the women in Dickens' novels until I read more about the women in his life: Elizabeth, the mother from whom he felt alienated; Fanny, the talented sister who died of consumption at thirty-eight; Maria Beadnell, the flirt who made him miserable in youth and again in middle age; Mary, the beloved sister-in-law who expired in his arms at eighteen and haunted his dreams for a long time after; Catherine his lady wife, who was neither as slovenly, as weak, nor as wearisome as critics – following Dickens' own lead – have made her; Ellen Ternan, the woman who came between Dickens and Catherine; and Georgina whom Dickens himself nicknamed "the Virgin", loyal and loving as any wife, but also a strong-willed individual.

When I first began to look for a suitable woman as the subject of a story, Georgina quickly distinguished herself. The first thing I read about her was that she had been suspected of having an affair with her famous brother-in-law, and that she had actually consulted a doctor to obtain a "certificate of virginity." What, I wondered, would bring a person to the point where she would submit to such an examination, especially in an age where women were supposed to be so modest about their sexuality?

The simple answer would seem to be: she did it out of loyalty to Dickens himself. Michael Slater sums up the immense attachment she had for her brother-in-law:

> She became practically and emotionally indispensable to him. After his death – his last conscious breath was drawn in her arms – Georgina lived on for over forty 'widowed' years, her existence deriving its point and purpose from her long, intimate association with the great man. She fretted over the depressing lives of his unsatisfactory children, consoling herself by drawing closer to the one indubitable success among them, the sixth son, Henry Fielding Dickens; and she worked to keep 'the

> Beloved Memory' properly venerated and untarnished before the world. (Slater 164)

And Dickens apparently thought just as highly of her. For he wrote the "Violated Letter" (quoted in entirety by Slater 373-5) in defense, not of Ellen Ternan, but of Georgina, whose reputation had been besmirched by salacious rumours of incest.

However, I think she had her own reasons for submitting to this strange test of loyalty. She was not a plaster saint like Agnes Wickfield, nor a disgruntled spinster like Fanny Squeers. Georgina was a strong and independent woman who dared to flout the dictates of society to get what she wanted out of life. She chose to remain single in an age when a woman was expected to marry. With her own hands she carved herself a niche in Dickens' household, and stayed there, in spite of opposition from her family and the ugly rumours circulating in society.

I felt that the story of Georgina Hogarth's virginity test was a remarkable detail that deserved to be remembered, as an index – indeed as a testament – to her character and to her role in Charles Dickens' life.

Bibliography

Ackroyd, Peter. *Dickens*. London: Sinclair-Stevenson, 1990.

Adrian, Arthur. *Georgina Hogarth and the Dickens Circle*. London: Oxford University Press, 1957.

Ames, Jonathan. "The Literary Dick (as in Private Detective)." 2004. URL: http://www.jonathanames.com/blog/archive/literary/2004_03_28_archive.html. (I am indebted to Ames for the expression "Certificate of virginity," which first sparked my interest in Georgina Hogarth, but the site is no longer maintained.)

Baird, John D. "Divorce and "Matrimonial Causes": An Aspect *of Hard Times*," *Victorian Studies* 20 (1977): 401 – 412.

Cool Nurse. "Pelvic Exams." 2000. URL: http://www.coolnurse.com/pelvic_exams.htm.

Dickens, Charles. *David Copperfield*. New York: New American Library, 1962.

—. "The Four Sisters." *Sketches by Boz*. Ed. Dennis Walder. Harmondsworth: Penguin, 1995. 29—34.

—. *Hard Times*. New York: Oxford University Press, 1998.

—. "The Magic Fishbone." In Vol. 15 of The Works of Charles Dickens. Boston: Houghton Mifflin, 1922. 409—418.

—. *Nicholas Nickleby*. Ed., introd. Michael Slater. Rev. ed. Harmondsworth: Penguin, 1982.

—. *The Old Curiosity Shop*. Ed. Angus Easson. Harmondsworth: Penguin, 1972.

—. *Pictures from Italy*. New York: William H. Colyer, 1846.

Fielding, K. J. "Dickens and the Hogarth Scandal." *Nineteenth-Century Fiction* 10 (1955-1956): 64 – 74.

Horstman, Allen. *Victorian Divorce*. New York: St. Martin's Press, 1985.

Hughey, M. J. "Pelvic Exam." 2003. Winnetka, IL: Medical Education Division, Brookside Associates Ltd. URL: http://www.brooksidepress.org/Products/ Military_OBGYN/Textbook/GynecologicExam/Pelvic/pelvicexam.htm

Intuition Communication Ltd. "Harley Street Guide." 2005. URL: http://www.harleystreetguide.co.uk/about/.

Peacock, John. *Costume 1066 to the Present*. Rev. ed. London: Thames and Hudson, 1994.

Perdue, David. "David Perdue's Charles Dickens Page." Created 1997 and last updated June 4, 2012. URL: http://charles-dickenspage.com. (See especially the links to "Family and Friends" and "Dickens London Map.")

Pierce, Ray Vaughn. *The People's Common Sense Medical Adviser in Plain English or, Medicine Simplified*. 54th ed. Buffalo, NY: World's Dispensary Printing Office and Bindery, 1895.

Pool, Daniel. *What Jane Austen Ate and Charles Dickens Knew: From Fox Hunting to Whist – the Facts of Daily Life in 19th – Century England*. New York: Touchstone, 1993.

Rathe, Richard. "Examination of the Female Pelvis." Created Aug. 1 1996 and modified Dec. 19 2000. Gainesville, Fla.: University of Florida. URL: http://medinfo.ufl.edu/year1/bcs/clist/pelvic.html

Rose, Phyllis. "Catherine Hogarth & Charles Dickens: 1835 – 1858." *Parallel Lives: Five Victorian Marriages*. New York: Vintage Books, 1984, pp. 141 – 191.

Slater, Michael. *Dickens and Women*. Stanford, Calif.: Stanford University Press, 1983.

Stone, Lawrence. *Road to Divorce: England, 1530-1987*. Oxford: Oxford University Press, 1990.

Wilbur, C. Keith. Antique Medical Instruments. 3rd ed. Atglen, Pa: Schiffer Pub. Co., 1998.

Willison, Marjory. *The Golden Treasury of Famous Books: A Guide to Good Reading for Boys and Girls and for the Enjoyment of Those who Love Books*. Toronto: Macmillan, 1929.

MRS. LOUIS RIEL

Pauline Hewak

Forgive me, Father, for I have sinned. It has been two weeks since my last confession.

I am grateful that you would hear my confession, my last, I think, God have mercy on me and my little babes. I could not come to you – my consumption makes me so weak and I do not leave this room now. My children are brought to me each day for a little time, just long enough for me to hold their tiny hands and look into their eyes. Jean, my eldest, is dark like his father and Marie-Angelique is fair with blue eyes. I have heard it whispered that she looks like Evelina, the woman Louis had been betrothed to in Montana a long time ago, before me. I wonder if Louis thought so too. My mother-in-law, Julie, found her letters, kept all these years, with Louis' papers.

Father, I have sinned and my faith has been weakened because of it. My sin is anger – anger against my life, against Louis, too, God rest his poor, tormented soul. It must be difficult for you to understand my life, living here in Winnipeg, far from Batoche. But, forgive me … I … I forgot for a moment. Nothing is left there. All is burned to the ground, except for the church of St. Antoine de Padoue, and the rectory. But that was not my home, not my real home. My real home was at Fort Ellice, on the Manitoba-Saskatchewan border where my family had moved after I was born in Red River, Manitoba. Like many Métis, my family followed the buffalo, and we ended up in Montana. We elected Louis chief and that is how I came to know him.

Father, I do not want to be disrespectful to Louis' memory. I have too much time alone, lying here in the dark. I have been dreaming of when I was a girl and it makes me sad for how I once was – so hopeful, so devout. It was thought that I would go into the convent and I had wanted that for myself. But after much prayer I had a strong dream – I thought it must be God Himself who urged me to accept my parents' plan for me to marry Louis. And so I did.

Poor Louis – the others taunted him. Perhaps it was because he seemed, by his manner, to be above all humanness. I think he surprised them. My friends wondered at my choice. Louis was so serious, so driven and so unlike my father, who was called Bellehumeur, although his real name was Monet. Louis was a hero to many because of Red River and I did not think that even I could match him in religious devotion. I put my trust in God and we married in April of 1881. I had hoped that we would grow old together, although, I must tell you, Father, I had fears even then. Our way of life was in peril and perhaps that is why we as a people were so desperate. My time with Louis was to be short – only five years.

I was happiest when we were in Montana, although we were poor and work was difficult to find. Louis did all kinds of labouring jobs, like all Métis men. He cut wood, hauled freight, hunted buffalo; he traded a little bit, and he did, for a while, even sell liquor. He taught school for a short time, but working the long hours took him away from his writing, his prayer and his work. I was a housekeeper and took care of my babies.

Louis was obsessed with the plight of our people, and that of our Native brothers. He became more involved in politics. Once he was charged with election fraud, which caused him great stress. Like always, Louis was helped by those who believed in him, or pretended to believe in him.

When Louis traveled back to see his family in St. Vital for his sister's wedding, he used the opportunity to look into the business of his land that he'd been trying to sell. He was not fearful of being arrested, because ten years had passed since the Rebellion and Thomas Scott's execution, but I was full of worry. There were always stories of plots by the Orangemen to assassinate him, and if Louis did not live in fear I often did. I prayed that God would protect him.

I confess that I was not always a good wife, Father. I worked very hard to take care of my family, and I bless my parents for having taught me the ways of our people. In every place that we lived, I relied on my homemaking skills. Not the kinds of skills that girls might learn in

Winnipeg, but those that girls who follow the buffalo with their men would need to know. It wasn't in that regard I was lacking. I was lacking in faith, Father, faith in God and faith in my husband.

Sometimes he seemed so detached from the world that I feared he was losing his mind. He loved me and the children – that I know – but he was so despondent over his government dealings that he sometimes spent days locked in his room, praying and writing letters. Louis wrote numerous letters with many drafts. Some he never sent. Some I burned. Others, I think have been kept by his secretary, Henri Jaxon. I wonder what has happened to those letters. I would try to calm him through the door, reminding him about how much he was doing for his people, and how much they relied on him to speak for them. But I will admit that I, too, began to fear that Louis was pushing too hard. Louis had many enemies, too.

Father, I am tired, and I know that God sends for me. My consolation is that I will see Louis once again. We will speak of the children, of course, and of our families, and old friends like Father André and Gabriel Dumont. I miss them both. Father André was, they told me, so overcome with grief on the scaffold that his legs gave way. Gabriel is like Michael the Archangel, Father, although it might seem irreverent to say so. He was the one who came looking for me and the children after Batoche. He found us in a cave where the men had hidden us, cold and hungry. We did not know where Louis was then. I cried and cried when they told me that Louis refused to run away to the American side like some of the others, Jaxon and later Gabriel among them.

Father, Canadian scouts found Louis walking along a path to meet them, wearing a Hudson Bay blanket, a misshapen Stetson and a white handkerchief tied around one sleeve.

During his imprisonment and his trial I was housebound due to my illness. I received many letters from Louis. His message was always the same – take heart, because God is guiding us. Father – Louis sent me a letter on the day of his execution. It told me to take care of the children, for they belong to God more than to me. He wrote that sometimes the saddest days are the most agreeable for God. How does one understand a man like that, Father?

Perhaps my sin is that I did not try hard enough. In his will he thanked me for being loyal and loving, but I weep when I hold his letters now. I cannot read them, Father. I cannot read at all. There is no time to learn to read when one is following the buffalo. All those letters were read to me by others. Louis knew that would be the case. I wonder if he held back because of it.

He did not know how much I suffered during those long absences from him, the times I resented all the meetings with farmers and Natives and Métis that went long into the night. I did not let him know, Father, because he believed that this was the role with which God had burdened him and, as his wife, I could not stand in the way.

On that terrible, final day, November 16, 1865, a date I wonder if anyone will remember, Louis was welcomed by God into heaven. I did not go – how could I stand it? Father André told me that Louis had been dismayed at the worn state of the clothes they gave him to wear on that morning. Father, I weep and weep to know that. When I met him he was handsome and well-groomed and the photograph I hold in my hand shows it to be so. He had moccasins on his feet, on that scaffold.

He was calm, Father André said. That knowledge helped me bear the next few days. When they finally released his body after many weeks, a procession carried the poor wooden casket to his mother's house. I wept in shame that he should be treated in such a manner. We gave him a new coffin that sat in Julie's house beside a little altar. For two days the people streamed through. I can hardly remember it, I was so sick. I lay on the couch beside the coffin as the mourners came. I prayed that God would take me away too, but I am still here, these five months later. I think, now, Father, that God has heard me. Louis will be waiting to see me, don't you think, Father?

I worry about my children. The men say that they will always be taken care of. I must put my trust in God. Let them grow strong, and remember their maman, who cared for them and loved them more than her own life. Most importantly, they must remember their father, Louis David Riel, who blesses them and all of the Métis and Natives who continue to suffer for the land and for their way of life. History will tell his story, and the people will remember.

You are quiet, Father.

Tell me that it is so.

Author's Note

I wrote this piece as an assignment for a writing course. The subject matter came easily to me because I have been intrigued by Louis Riel since I was a young woman. Our family travelled to Regina, Saskatchewan, the place of my father's birth, as a kind of homecoming for him in 1972.

Regina had an allure because my father often told us stories of his hard-scrabble life as the child of Ukrainian immigrants. Interwoven with stories of his youth – when some men still wore buffalo hide coats – were stories of Native heroes and warriors, and brave dogs like Silver Chief. Sometimes we cried at bedtime because a hunter was trapped under the ice, only to be found by his lover in the spring. Other times we went to bed happy when a sled dog saved the day. For us the West was magical.

While in Regina we attended a reenactment of Louis Riel's trial, in the original courtroom where he was sentenced to hang. My parents and four siblings – the youngest only seven years old – were deeply moved by the experience. We all wept. I have never forgotten his last request: that a sack of flour be given to his wife so that she and his children could eat. I am quite certain that much of my interest in Native history and art stems from that experience.

A few years ago my husband and I took our daughter across Canada and we did our own Louis Riel pilgrimage. We visited the former village and battlefield site at Batoche, Saskatchewan. We stood at Louis's grave in the cemetery at St. Boniface Cathedral in Winnipeg. We quietly toured his mother's house in St. Vital, Manitoba, where his wife Marguerite had long ago rested on the couch beside his coffin, six months before her own death from tuberculosis and a broken heart. I wanted to feel her presence then, but could not. Her story haunts me still.

THE CHANGELING

Joe Girard

Are you a witch, or are you a fairy?
Or are you the wife of Michael Cleary?

Betterment is rare with age. I watch God's ever-grey ocean bite away at Ireland's proud cliffs, felling her green trees, and mouldering her vibrant grasses yellow, balding new rocks for the eating. I watch it lick the hull of this boat as we strive feebly westward, toward a fallen sun, subject as all things are to the ocean's bottomless appetites, its glittering jaws swallowing all light, night after black night.

Betterment. God created heaven and earth not to better it, but to find entertainment in the slow decay of His perfection. Beauty he built to crinkle, joy to darken, family to dismantle, and memory to fog. Memory. Our lamp in the fog at times and the fog itself at others, vanishing from my aging mind as nimbly as a child swipes away a spider's wearying work. One must choose carefully what they hold onto as the facts are smudged out round the centre.

I hold onto a story. This story.

I hold onto a name. Michael Cleary. The man who murdered my cousin. The man they released after half a sentence served. The man who fled to Canada to escape a people with a memory.

I hold onto a place. Ballyvadlea. A hilly township of south Tipperary, where God allowed our superstitions to disembowel its quiet, lonesome beauty, unimaginably now to city-folk well-versed in our tragedy.

I hold onto a face. Bridget's. Young and lovely, arresting and divine. The sort of face passing travellers have recalled in homes and taverns throughout all Tipperary and beyond as long as I've lived. The sort of face none would imagine at rest in the marriage bed of a man as sullen and odious as Michael Cleary. The sort of face that clogged the path to her home daily with ineligible suitors.

I know. I fought my way through such a cloud of young musk that day in 1887, returning home from the Lady Margaret Hall at Oxford, having taken American literature studies. I came home at twenty-seven years of age, to find my nineteen year old cousin a vision of God's grandeur. Crimson waves of hair, falling in intricate rivers around eyes blazing hazel in the morning light, her pouting cherry lips in an impish grin. But her beauty only served to mask a fierce capacity. Already self-taught in the art of dressmaking, her Singer sewing machine was one of the first in our county, and the first I'd ever lain my own eyes upon. An impressive device it was, shaped like a gun, crafted of sleek black iron, with a sophisticated mechanism for punching stitches, jumping in and out of a piece of cloth with a lively, musical rhythm. Like Bridget, it promised a bright, prosperous future. But such is not God's view of His world.

"Cousin Hannie!" she cried, seeing me at the gate, wreathed by boys on their best behaviour. At once I understood why these boys were so unabashedly desperate, and almost forgave them their insufferable behaviour, barking into their sleeves at me to take pity and steal one along. Bridget blew all the other maids away, despite their abundance in those days. Men had their pick, and most picked Bridget. Describing beauty is a vain task best left to the poets, I say. Still, if Bridget had been born in Rome, would there be any end to the, I say, impossible task of containing her infectious effervescence in paint or stone? It's no wonder she bore as many enemies as she did, both amongst the envious and the lustful.

She closed the door on the boys and leaned against it, shaking her head playfully as she said, "Philistines, no doubt. Every last one of them. Not a one could my heart ensnare, let alone father's."

I laughed. "My parents let you have your way with my library, I see. Philistines, indeed. What's wrong with one of them, anyway? You've got your pick of the lot, you realize."

"A woman's husband and father drink at the same tavern," she said, enigmatically. I could already tell we were going to be fast friends. She grinned a grin that said she'd all but married some bloke already, and I crossed my arms at her, waiting. "So … you might well say … Michael Cleary's your uncle's younger self."

My heart sank. Maybe it was my years at Lady Margaret Hall, which had left me desiring fewer Patrick Boland's on this earth. Maybe it was his feverish attachment to superstition, or his own marriage to Bridget's mother, Bridget Boland, known throughout the land as a slieveen. A fairy doctor. One versed in the folklore and known to consort with the fairy realm. A trickster, I say. Either way, I disliked Bridget's choice.

Still, how better could one explain Bridget's affection for such a sullen man as Michael, when her own bouncing, frolicking laughter sang like music across Ballyvadlea? Of all the women brutally murdered from Joan of Arc – rest her sainted soul – onward, none of them wed Bridget's other suitors. It's another cruel jape of His to raise Bridget under Patrick's stern tutelage, making her wet-lipped for Michael's morose kisses.

"Michael's a weed trying to grow up between sunflowers," I said.

"Laffy-daffy sunflowers, maybe. Juvenile greenery that wouldn't know how to blossom if the sun shone right in their baby faces."

"Michael's no baby, sure he isn't. He's older than me, Bridget. He's moody, and the man practically absorbs the light around him. He comes to sit in my library at times – "

"Which is where we first met, thanking you kindly."

" – quietly mulling over … what? He's a cooper, for pity's sake. What's a cask-maker got to mull over? Besides the difference twixt a butter churn and a hogshead."

Michael was a difficult man to describe, and one I would rather have put from mind in those days. Reading was a gift God allowed him, but not proper speech. Lucky as a rich gambler, he was, yet was often behind on his payments. I abided his presence in my home, and later, at Bridget's side, for the simple reason that he'd never hurt a fly, so far as I knew. She loved him, why shouldn't I? His broad shoulders, his dark eyes, his black shock of hair, all seemed to collect the shadows inward. He was the still water in the glen, a small surface masking unspeakable depths.

In talk, his words were choice and few. "Han, what say you of selkies?"

"Water-hags of myth," I answered, without care.

"What of trolls, Han?"

"A tale to frighten children, Michael. To put a parent's thoughts at ease, letting their young ones out to field." I laughed. "We've had thirty years to discover these beasties under their rocks, behind their trees, beyond their waterfalls. Don't you think you'd have seen at least one crop up by now, Michael?"

"What of fairies? Of wizards? Goblins, Han?"

He was of single mind.

Bridgie managed to make her way in the city, a dressmaker's assistant of top repute, beloved by anyone that good fortune brought to the shop. But her mother's failing health lured her back to the countryside where Michael decided to leave her, preferring himself to stay in the city. She took to visiting with old suitors, until Michael took to jealousy. I told her I suspected guilt drove him to the odd notion and she just nodded and sighed, "He's making a fairy of me, Han."

Anyone would tell you, she only meant to say he was pushing her away. But her words took on a sinister darkness in the weeks to come.

I should've seen it coming. Should've known Michael's worst qualities were being brought out by that house. Built where an old rath once stood – that being a fairy fort, a circle of stones the superstitious believe to be a meeting place for the Good Folk – the place had driven out its prior occupant with strange noises he took to be the shrieks of angry fairies. Everyone knew the place to be of ill omen. A reputation such as drove the price right into the market of a newly wedded couple like Michael and Bridget. Course, they still couldn't get in, as the home was the finest in the land at that time. Large, lofty, and modern. It was designated for labourers only. And that's how Patrick Boland, a labourer in his lost youth, came to live with Bridget.

1894. A time of crippled wallets for most folks. So even though she slaves away at that Singer in her bedroom, and even though her prices beat the city fares hand over fist, lots of folks couldn't cough up the coin. And with Michael's living abroad ... to nail his casks ... the star-crossed couple fell into arrears.

Accompanied her, I did, on a few collections. To see the sad, embarrassed, weary look on the faces of them too poor to meet even the modest sum as was Bridget's fee, well, tis not a mood one wishes on one's enemies. Sweet a sweetheart as she was, Bridget let the trouble slide more often than not, at her own expense.

If only I'd been with her that day she went up Kylenagranagh Hill to face Jack Dunne, the old, thinning, drunkard slieveen, with more first-hand fairy stories in his pocket than coin. He'd been off getting stewed with that wife of his, while Bridget braved the freezing rain of that chill November to traverse the unswept, unkept paths, and bang at the door of Jack's empty hovel. Well, he never did pay her the due coin. But after she returned home, like death warmed over, shivering uncontrollably by the fire we built for her, sicker than the sickest dog, a hair's breadth from death's bony clutch, he bothered himself to pay her a visit. To proclaim, "That is not Bridget Boland."

She repeated the words to me from her sickbed, bitter and angry. " 'That is not Bridget Boland.' " she intoned, mimicking Jack's false gravity. "Then I suppose you needs not pay me, hey, Jack?"

"Ol' Jack Dunne couldn't pay a beggar to follow him to a tavern." I mused.

"Aye," she croaked, paling as she spoke. "Just the barman."

"Aye," I said, chuckling bitterly. Then I changed the subject, as Jack's name only seemed to make Bridget paler. "What did Dr. Crean have to say about you?"

"Bronchitis, says he. Medicine and bed rest, and I'll be back on my feet." She closed her eyes and sighed again. I don't think I'd ever heard her sigh in earnest, before those final days. "That's assuming Michael or Dada choose to ever give me the doctor's medicine – instead of the foxglove Denis Ganey gave them, to drive out the 'unearthly creatures' inside me. Can you believe, my own Michael thinks me inhuman?"

Remembering our many talks on the subject of the supernatural, I well understood that Michael belonged to the old way of thinking, and that, yes, it was more than believable he'd stake his claim on Bridget being overtaken by fairy-kind.

But could I bring myself to tell her that? After all, it was I who provided Michael with the virgin cow's milk Denis Ganey said was needed to activate the curative properties in his foxglove remedy. Was I not an accomplice to the madness? Did I not watch as Father Ryan, our own good priest, and Jack Dunne and Patrick Boland forced it down her throat? Did I not hear Michael say with his own lips, "She is not my wife at all but a fairy-thing from Kylenagranagh Hill ..." and keep my peace? Ten years I'd been married. Sure, I knew a thing or two about men's ways. Enough to stay out of them. If only staying out of it was something Bridget permitted.

"A woman's husband and father drink at the same tavern," I said, finally. "You told me that at the beginning, and you're right. Michael thinks as Patrick does. And as your mother did. He has none of your forward thinking at all."

Bridget seemed to consider that a moment. But the sun fell behind a cloud and the room plunged into shadow. "Dada looked into my eyes. My own father. And he screamed, Han. He screamed 'Are you Bridget Boland, daughter of Patrick Boland, wife of Michael Cleary?' And I tried to tell them yes, yes, yes, I'm Bridget, I'm the one you've loved, I'm the one you've raised, the one you've spared from childbirth, the one you've left to slave away in solitude on a fairy hill in Ballyvadlea, like a godforsaken spinster. It's me. Have you forgotten me? What must I needs do to prove my guts and my soul are the ones God gave me? Tear them out and throw them at your feet? I'll do it!"

Then, at the edge of her bed, she crumpled into my arms, like a tumbling-down barn, and wept. I wanted to lift her spirits, but all I could think to say was, "Stories such as yours, my dear, they're the pest flies about the trash of Irish history. You have to promise to raise your own without filling their heads with such nonsense. Michael married you, after all, didn't he? Not a slieveen like your own mother, rest her soul."

She did calm, but then said, "It is a horrific thought. I understand the horror of it. Your wife of seven years, suddenly transformed, swapped for an imitation, a forgery. A changeling. Oh, God be good, he's calling me a changeling, Han."

"A changeling?" Could Michael be that far gone? I wondered.

"It's envy, he says, that draws the fairies to a person. Other people envying you. And what's not to envy about me, Han? My business, my home, my godforsaken face. But if they only knew my husband ... who calls me … who's decided I'm inhuman." She turned worried eyes on me, as if she'd just realized something. "Do you envy me, Han?"

"Not with the man you're after marrying," I said. "I don't think I'll ever forgive myself if I envy you after this black day." I smiled a smile I hoped was reassuring. But in my mind I knew it was never envy playing the thin edge of the wedge between Bridgie and me, but wrath. The loathsome scorn I was feeling about her bringing me between a man and wife. That's no place for anyone, let alone a cousin.

She tried to smile back at me. "But I've heard stories, Han." The water welled up in those hazel eyes again. "Mothers roasting their babies on hot shovels, new brides thrown over cliffs, all because someone calls out, 'changeling!' And what's a changeling? They're just tales! Don't people understand? They're just bedtime stories! What does he mean to say his wife is a changeling? Does he want to hold *me* on a hot shovel? Toss *me* over a cliff?"

If only.

Before the rotten business of 'curing' Bridget was set in motion, Michael appeared in my library, pacing the room, flipping through books on fairy culture and on medicine, sitting and standing, sitting and standing. What was he looking for in those old Irish accounts? Some historic anecdote to salve his suspicions? How could any book gainsay such an ironclad faith?

"I'm afeared, Han," he said, already a far more verbose man than normal. "Afeared I won't have the strength to do it. The strength to do what God needs I do. To do what has to be done."

"I'm afeared you will have the strength, Michael." That gave him pause, and the look he shot me was deadly cold, like a fox sensing a lame rabbit. "What is it you think God needs of you?"

He resumed his pacing, but began raking his scalp with fingernails soon gone ruddy. "It's not murder if it's Bridget on the Hill … if them so-called Good Folk switched her for a *changeling!* I know they did! If her mother were alive, she'd tell you. They switched her!"

Without thinking, I moved behind my tall-backed reading chair and said, "No beast or fowl under God goes to its death unmurdered if it's a human hand as laid the killing blow."

"Not if she's on the Hill!" he shrieked, grabbing one of my books with a now-bloody hand and throwing it at my fire pit, missing. "Jack Dunne knows! He's a slieveen. He consorts with them, don't you know it? Don't you know anything, Han? Jack Dunne knows. He's my friend. He's there right now, bargaining for Bridget's life. My sweet ..."

It was a pitiful sight, I'll admit, watching Michael Cleary cry. Still, I remained where I was, behind the reading chair. "What does God require of you in this black time, Michael?" I asked, wondering if Father Ryan would ask the same question. "Is it to follow Jack Dunne and Patrick Boland down their dark path? Are their words the words of God, Michael? What if they aren't? What will you tell God when He asks you why you took their word over His own?"

He was hunched over by then, his dark wave of hair tumbling over his face. "Damn you, Johanna Burke! It's not my wife, but a beast from beyond the Hill. A bitch-witch who's tricked even you. With all your books." He spat.

Scared as a child, but strong as a woman, I braved the unspoken truth. "'He's making a fairy of me.' Why did Bridget say, 'He's making a fairy of me,' Michael? We know what that means. You! Only coming home on the weekends for your own sick wife. Who's sharing your bed, Michael? Do you not love your wife, Michael? Have you not a soul in you, Michael? You never should have entered that house – "

And just like that the words were out of me and in the air between us, heavy and deadly as a lion. I bit my tongue, knowing what I'd inspired.

"Aye," he said indignantly, looking back up at me, "the house. The bloody, rath-be-cursed house! Built on a circle of fairy-cursed stone – damn us both, for living there a day. A portal for bringing devilry and witchcraft – "

"No."

" – and fairies – "

"*No!*"

" – and sorcery and mystery and evil and ... torture and suffering and good God I haven't slept eight nights, Han. Thinking, tossing, turning, wearied by endless evil spirits jabbing and stabbing – and that blasted rath! It's laughing at me from under the floorboards. I just want to sleep. But I can't. They took her from me. And I'm taking her *back*."

"You can't take back what hasn't been stolen, Michael!"

He looked at me incredulously. "You really … don't believe, do you? When O'Grady, the last bloke who lived there, left, what'd you think he escaped for? For fun? He left from the screaming, Han! The screaming banshees of the angry fairies what knew, *WHAT KNEW*, that no man nor woman – "

"Nor child …"

" – was meant to live there, *AND DON'T THINK I DON'T KNOW WHAT YOU MEAN!*"

I have to admit I embarrassed myself with that remark. It was a right unfit barb in the heat of that moment. Thankfully, Michael seemed to calm. "It's the best house in the vale, Han. You think it was easy us getting in there? It was reserved for labourers. If Patrick Boland hadn't been a labourer when he were younger, we'd never have bagged it."

In his calmer state, I decided to chance bringing Michael back to reason. "Michael … you're old enough to know … Slieveens aren't legitimate. They don't really talk to fairies, because fairies are folklore, Michael. They're like kelpies, joint-eaters, and merrows of old. They simply don't exist, and no one's ever seen one."

"You're a liar, Johanna Burke! With all your books. You don't know the first thing. You're a *damned LIAR!*"

With one thick hand he cascaded a row of books across the room, succeeding in landing one or two in the fire. I ran from behind the chair finally, to rescue them from irreversible damage. But I could already see the fall and the flames had done their dirty business. The books were torn and burnt beyond repair. And with my back turned Michael had triumphed in escaping the room without my notice.

When I finally ran after him, my broken books stored safely away, I found a trail of evening visitors leading right up to the Cleary house on Tullowcassuan Hill where screams and shouts emanated, recalling O'Grady's howling fairies.

Dr. Crean was on the trail, probably fresh from the tavern, stinking of the neck oil that was ruining his reputation.

Father Ryan was there, clutching his black book to his chest like a child's blanket, as though it would protect him against his deeds in our black affair.

I pushed through the bottlenecking crowd gathered at the front door, to see a sight to quell the town crier, as my own mother might've said of it. Seeing it stopped me at the fore of the crowd, else I might've charged straight into the pandemonium.

Wound in red-soaked bedclothes, Jack Dunne holding her head, Michael lifting her feet, and the man-child Patrick Boland at her arms, she hung in the air beside the blaze set on the hearth like a floating, thrashing spectre. It was enough, drenched in the last red rays of day, pouring over the heads of them staring through the windows, to put the fear of fairies into anyone's heart.

As for the hearth, it was choked with logs. Flames raced up the chimney, and spilled into the room, a mad smoke collecting in the rafters. My first thought was to save the house from burning down. But the place was indeed impressively modern, and the stone chimney contained the scrabbling arms of orange heat.

Their neighbour, Tom Smith, a stockier man than Michael, with fair red hair, and crystal blue eyes, was the only man within the lofty main hall, bless his soul, who seemed to be trying to stop the madness. But whenever he made a move toward the three men dropping Bridget on the floor, Jack Dunne shot him a fierce look, baring his crooked teeth. "Looks like we got ourselves a fairy sympathizer, men!" Jack said. "I know all about them. Foolish folk who've forgotten the old ways. The fairies will come for him sooner or later, you'll see. Trade his own self for a changeling. See what he thinks about fairy magic then."

Tom, seeing Bridget plain and true, cried, "She's only middling, Michael! You're making a fairy out of her!"

The words terrified me with their potency, and I could see in the eyes of those gathered a similar dread. Unfortunately, the words only seemed to spur on the men inside to their purpose. Weak-boned Patrick Boland, his white hair a shock of orange flame in the firelight, began intoning, in his feverish voice, "Are you the daughter of Patrick Boland, wife of Michael Cleary?"

Those damn words again.

"I am, Dada!" poor Bridget screamed.

Again he asked, and again she assured him. A third time, and Bridget made no response. Was she sick of the charade? Was she sick of being doubted? Or was she just plain sick? Whatever the case, it proved to be reason enough for them to force more of Denis Ganey's potion down her throat. Some popped and spittled out of her mouth and Jack Dunne called out, "Look! Her body's refusing the medicine! It's fairy magic!"

"Oh, Han! Han!" Bridget wailed when she caught sight of me.

Michael, not quite as convinced as Dunne, saw me in the doorway and decided I was the one to blame. "Ganey's medicine was fine. It was that high and mighty bitch over there, Johanna Burke, who couldn't do one simple thing, and *FETCH ME THE RIGHT MILK FOR THE JOB!*"

Did Jack Dunne smirk? Did Patrick Boland wonder for a moment then if he might be squeezing the life out of his own daughter's wrists, as she struggled on the floor, the hearth flame behind her raging, inviting her inside with its reaching orange tendrils? Did the crowd dissipate then from shame, or from fear? We'll never know, I suppose, for I burst into the room then to put an end to it. But as I approached the scene, Michael took the poker from the fire pit and brandished it at me. I stopped dead in my step. Then he turned and dragged the poker across Bridget's face.

The heat hissed into her soft flesh, and Bridget's sick, tired eyes, rounded and bulged as pain forked into her. Her bellow of agony made everyone take a step back, even them at the windows. Most of us had to look away. But Michael's shouts brought us back.

"Out, devil!" The quiet, sullen young man of my library was gone. In his place stood a hysterical bully. "Out, you fairy wretch! Go on! Up the chimney with you! That's what you do, isn't it? Change! Change! Change!" He lashed Bridget with the red hot spear. Then he grabbed a piece of burning wood and pushed it in her face. Bridget wailed, trying in vain to move her head out of the way. He seemed to be trying to force her to eat it. Then he stripped her body bare but for a white chemise. My words died in my throat, dry and useless as dust on the road. Patrick and Jack recoiled, embarrassed to be restraining a half-naked woman, no doubt. And Bridget lay there in shame, unmoving, thinking the worst was over, I'll bet.

Michael began pacing again, stalking the lofty main hall with the poker in hand. Tom Smith was the first one he moved at, and the smaller man was cowed into the kitchen. Next, Michael moved at them as watched through the windows and doors and like cattle they too were repelled, as if by some magic.

I watched it with disbelief. An entire crowd unable to stop one man. But when he came near me, I too quailed, stumbling backward to the nearest doorway, which turned out to be their bedroom, where Bridget had fought her illness for over a week. Michael continued circling the main hall in his dark silence.

A curious feeling swam through me then. Anger. Anger that Bridget had drawn me into this situation. I know what a wife's place is in the home, and I didn't intend to come out between man and wife. I promised myself I would stay the night to ensure Bridget's safety, but when I got a good look at the bedroom, I realized exactly how uncertain that safety truly was. It was a still view of the carnage they'd visited upon Bridget before her journey to the hearth flame. White oil soaked the bed sheets, the ceiling, the floor. It smelled like paraffin. I ignored that for a moment to pick the Singer sewing machine off the floor. It was in several pieces. Did Jack Dunne smash it, to show what he thought of his debt to Bridget? Or did Michael smash it, hoping he just might bring out the Bridget in his changeling?

Regardless, it was coated in the same paraffin-smelling wax as everything else, and I suddenly realized what was in Michael's mind to do.

"Give me a chance!" I heard Bridget cry out before I felt the loud *thump* of her head on the floorboards.

I summoned what strength I had left and re-entered the hearth-room to find Michael locking the doors, forcing the remaining onlookers to the windows for their vision of the bedlam. The roaring flames, the billowing smoke, the shifting shadows as Jack, Patrick, and Michael paced in circles around Bridget's little lump of flesh and bone, like jackals.

Was she dead? I weighed the point and purpose of risking mine own life to save her, if her soul had already found God's dark embrace. I looked to Smith, who was dancing on the spot with nervous energy. Michael had locked him inside with us, and other than myself, he was, no doubt, Bridget's only hope. He was the only one of the townsfolk I heard confronting Michael. Maybe he had a shot.

"For the love of God, Michael, don't burn your wife!" Smith found it in himself to say, keeping his distance. He obviously didn't believe

Bridget to be Michael's changeling, but something made him too craven to restrain the other men.

"I'll run you through!" Michael cried, stabbing the air before Smith with a knife. My eyes flared. Where did that knife come from? Thin air? "I'll roast you with her! That's your wish, hey? That's your wish?"

He then grabbed the burning log again and stuck it to his wife. It only took a moment for the chemise to catch and cling to Bridget's skin as it seared away her flesh.

"Bridgie is burned!" Smith whimpered loudly, perhaps aiming to alert the ones outside. The smoke filling the room dogged those still silhouettes watching through the windows, but at the sound of Smith's voice, they animated with concern. Was no one seeking the police? Perhaps they were all too agog. Perhaps some of them were the police. I could hear them asking themselves, as even I was, in some shadowed corner of my mind, if Michael was about to prove before our very eyes that the Good Folk were real, as he'd always suspected.

Then, as if he weren't human at all, but some curious Martian out of a Burroughs science fiction, Michael stopped pacing, turned calmly, looked at me and said, "Hannah, I believe she is dead." His voice was guiltless as a babe, and I almost cried with fury. Fury at Michael for his beliefs, fury at Bridget for being so damn pretty she could've had any man and choosing a right devil. Fury at the townsfolk for doing nothing. But the burnt lump of flesh and bone by the hearth soon stirred, and Michael was assured once more, restored for one final hope that what he did was the right thing, the only thing one could do.

He took up the lamp again and walked casually around her, letting out ropes of paraffin to splash over her body, black smoke issuing all around him, up through his clothes, and clouding darkly round his face. How he withstood it, I've no idea. Even Patrick and Jack were backing away, toward the open portal to the kitchen, coughing into their sleeves. Bridget, I could see, was gasping weakly as oil trickled over her face, and into her mouth.

Michael went to burn her with his log, and that was when I could take no more. I hurled myself at him, pushing through the soup of brown-grey fog to shove Michael into the window. Such that the townsfolk recoiled for a moment. "What are you doing with the creature?" I roared, unleashing my righteous fury, fighting to keep the whimper in my heart out of my voice. "Is it roasting her you are? Your own bleeding wife, Michael? This smog is the only thing going up that chimney tonight! She's not going to change! I know you want her to, but she's not! She never had!"

But before he could answer, Bridget moved on the floor, crawling for the front door, reminding us how badly she fought for life in those final moments.

Michael didn't miss his chance. "Are you Bridget Boland, wife of Michael Cleary?"

As she crawled, worse than a starved man meeting the end of his strength, lost in the desert, bound to a dream of life, one word escaped her wax-crusted, heat-scorched lips in a pitiful gasp: "Yes."

I can't describe how my heart lurched in that instant. My cousin, my best friend of so many years had reached up from the depths of pain, suffering, sickness, misery, and, no doubt, righteous indignation … and saved herself.

Michael, however, was of single mind.

He knifed his stick into the pool of oil. And Bridget brightened the room.

"For the love of God, Michael," Jack Dunne whispered at the kitchen door.

When Smith and I turned on Michael, who watched Bridget's un-transformed state with genuine surprise, he looked at us with shock. "She's not my wife!" he screamed, more at Smith than me, gesturing wildly at the corpse, smouldering on the floor. "She's an old deceiver sent in place of my wife. She's after deceiving me for the last seven or eight days and deceived the priest today too, but she won't deceive me any more. As I beginned with her, I will finish it with her. You'll soon see her go up the chimney!" He took to pacing around her again, as if that would inspire the changeling to finally give up the ghost and scamper away.

"Okay, Michael," Smith said, "just give us the key and we'll let ourselves out so you can finish with your business here."

"Ask me that again and you can join her," Michael replied calmly, tossing more ropes of oil across her burning carcass as he did.

Michael's hideous, vile-smelling work past the point of return, I fell back to the kitchen, where Boland and Dunne joined me, along with Smith. We all got down on the floor to get below the thickest of the brown-grey air, and the charred flakes of Bridget that hung, dancing in the air, like black leaves. Michael drew up a chair and sat down to watch Bridget burn, sporadically throwing on another rope of oil. His face was an orange mask, against the black shades in the windows, watching in silent horror.

After a time he called out, "You're a dirty set. You will rather have her with the fairies of Kylenagranagh then have her here with me?"

As if he didn't know what else to say to a man clearly beyond his wits, Patrick said, "If there's anything I can do to save my daughter, I'll do it."

In a moment of frightful calmness, Michael replied, "I'll bury her with her mother. Next Sunday I'll venture to Kylenagranagh. Bridget will appear to me on a white stallion. And if I can cut loose her bonds, she'll be mine again. Denis Ganey told me that. I believe Denis Ganey."

By then he had all but disappeared into the haze of smoke. Smith, in a fit of desperation, put his elbow through a window in the kitchen, and I watched, amazed, despite my exhaustion, as the black air swam out into the night sky, like a river of evil spirits.

When Michael came over to us afterward, and swore us to secrecy, we all agreed without hesitation. What did it mean, anyway, to pledge yourself to an insane man and his insane God? We all betrayed him in the end and Michael went away for fifteen years. Upon his early release, he boarded a boat for Montreal, where I'm headed now. He must think he can slip between the folds in the pages of history. But I've still got an ounce of strength left in me, and so help me I'll not give up the looking.

Author's Note

Bridget Boland first came to my attention when my girlfriend, Simone Deahl, was doing a school project on faeries and their cultural history. She told me a few stories concerning the generally insane and madcap goings-on surrounding faeries as a cultural staple. The one about Bridget jammed hard into the cogs of my faith in humanity, and likewise into my daily rotation of thoughts to ponder. I would like to thank my partner, Simone Deahl, my mother, Diane Girard, and Bernadette Rule for their invaluable help in lifting Bridget Boland's grievous story to full light.

NOON-DAY BRIGHT

Judy Pollard Smith

Surge Illuminare. "Arise, shine; for thy light is come."
Isaiah 60

The Congo, 1898

Alice awakes from another night of wrestling with shadows.

She reaches out for John. There is a slight coolness in the linen sheets where he should be. She hasn't heard him go. He would be off in the jungle for another four days, his Bible tucked under his arm, a guide and another missionary by his side. She misses him already.

She throws back the netting on the bed, lets her feet dangle over the side. Thick moist air clamps itself around her, a woolly, smothering glove.

Another day on the "Dark Continent", where Alice hopes to bring Light, will mean swarms of Filaria flies massing under her heavy skirts, tiny insects that cling to her glistening face to buzz in the loose tendrils of auburn hair, dampness that allows her wire-framed glasses to slip down her nose so that she can hardly see what she is doing.

She wishes she were like the Black Hippos, could submerge herself in the depths of the Congo River to keep hydrated under the brutal African sun, but then there would be crocodiles to deal with. Each spot in this hellish terrain has it own horrors. At times it is dense curtains of mosquitoes and gnats that threaten to be her undoing. At other times it is the darting thrust of a snake underfoot or the snuffling of a giant forest hog pushing its way past her as she forces her way through gnarled vines, over sucking mud.

She thinks of her parents' admonitions as she splashes the water from the bedside jug over her face.

Her father had said, "Under no condition will I give you leave to go! Whoever heard of a nineteen-year old girl wanting to go to the Congo? That is no place for any woman." He had shut himself off in his study and petitioned God to provide Alice with a husband, and soon.

Her mother had been equally implacable. "Why would you ever consider leaving us alone here in England as you go off into unknown terrors? You need the safety of a husband's arms, dear child."

In spite of her mother's tears, Alice had replied, "It isn't my will or yours that I intend to follow, Mother. It is God's will and His alone." She had left the room.

They had only relented when she had met and married Mr. John Harris, Baptist missionary, and together they had sailed off to the Congo.

And now, on this blazing morning, Alice pads across the floor to the small kitchen of the mission station. She is wondering about this new burden that has been placed upon her heart. Will today be another day of things she can no longer bear? If John were here, he would have some advice for her, some practical aid, but as it is she will have to cope on her own, will have to make what will prove to be a momentous decision for the history of this land.

Makemba has set out breakfast for her on a neat white cotton cloth: a banana, some pineapple, a bit of plantain. She pours the tea into the floral cup that she has brought from England with her. It trickles in an amber stream, splashes on bone china. She likes the simplicity of this daily routine. It reminds her of home, and of things that remain the same. Not so here, in this place where dazzling morning sun has fooled her into believing that all is bright; not so in this place where shadows can reconfigure even brilliant hours into a most lamentable dusk.

She sits, sips her tea, smiles at the small note John has left on the table for her. Her heart warms as she reads.

> *My own Alice,*
>
> *I will miss you, Dear. Makemba will stay with you. Nsala has promised me that he will watch out for you. I will be home in four days time. Pray God for my safekeeping Dear, and I shall pray for yours.*
>
> *Always, Your John*

It is then that she hears it, that sound that she has heard too many times this past fortnight. It begins as a distant wail, then comes closer, then so close that she is faced again with this new, darkening reality.

Then a scream. Makemba is calling to her from the porch of the Mission Station. "Come Mrs. Harris! Come!" Makemba shrieks. "It's Nsala! Come!"

Alice jolts, knocks the teacup off of the tiny table. It shatters.

Nsala is there, his ebony face screwed in pain. He is sobbing.

"What is it Nsala?" she asks. "Nsala! What is it?"

He places a small bundle on the porch in front of Alice. Her glasses are steamed and she cannot see. She wipes at them as she fingers the contents of the bundle to feel the hardening skin of what she soon recognizes to be a tiny human foot, a tiny human hand. Her fingers have memory. They have felt these cursed, clouded shapes before.

"Tell me everything, Nsala," Alice demands. She motions to his companions who stand near the porch pillars. "I must hear everything. Do you understand? Everything."

Nsala sinks onto the floor of the porch. He folds his head into his arms, weeping softly now. "It's my daughter, Mrs. Harris. The Belgians. The overseers. They say I haven't cut enough rubber vines. They punish me Mrs. Harris. They cut off my daughter's foot, her hand! She is only five years old Mrs. Harris. Why do they punish my baby girl? Next they say they'll take my hand, my foot if I don't cut more vines for them!"

Makemba brings juice, urges Nsala to drink. His companions stand nearby, form a circle around him as if to deflect more evil should it arrive again, as it so often does on this Mission Station porch.

She remembers her parents' gift to her, the gift that she has used over and over again this past month to document these horrors. Makemba is there already, has it in her hands. "Your camera, Mrs. Harris," she says softly.

It is a Kodak, one of the first cameras made for non-professional use. It had been a farewell gift from her parents. They couldn't have known how it would change things, for Nsala, for the others.

Click! Snap! Alice pulls a string to open the shutter, depresses the button to let in the light. It is always about light in this dark place, and now this. Click! Snap! Light pours in, shimmers in gritty corners, eclipses shadow.

Alice sends Makemba home with Nsala, asks his companions to fetch the nurse at the next Missionary Station and take her to Nsala's daughter. She knows what her job is. She must act now, not wait for John.

Alice goes back indoors, removes the cotton cloth from the table, pushes the teacup shards into the corner with her foot, gathers what she will need to do this job, to alter the way people see, to brighten the path.

Surge, Illuminare. Rise, Shine, for thy Light is come.

Her pile of photographs has grown this past month, a pile of things best unseen. And yet, she, Alice, has seen the toll the Belgian overseers are garnering from the enslaved Congolese men, women, children. She has been presented with many of these grim human tokens that are meant to impress a greedy Belgian King, these gifts for a cruel regime.

She spends the rest of the morning, then the afternoon, wrapping the photos. String, scissors, knives, jungle twine; all are used to secure the items, to keep the evil inside the wooden box she has saved for this purpose; a madwoman now, she is taping, tying, wrapping, pulling the twine tighter and tighter around each packet as if to strangle the life out of it, to end it. With care, the gloom will remain in the package until it is opened at its destination, revealing its sorrow under the watery sun of an English summer's day.

Shadows creep across the skyline as Alice hands the parcel to the shipping agent. Soon, inky darkness will drop like a curtain, will encroach upon every corner of this Mission Station; there will be no gleam of light, no air to breathe, no room for sighs. Sleep will be the only option.

"You must promise to take very good care of this package," Alice tells the Agent. "What is in here must reach London. It is a matter of life and death."

The Agent's eyes round, his face drips, his hot hands are shaking. She hands him a cup of pineapple juice. He gulps it, sets off to a neighbouring hut to sleep.

Alice is firm about her mission. She wants Belgium's King Leopold and his policy of blood-sucking Colonialism dealt with. How is Alice to guess that her package will create a stir in England that has not been felt since the Reformation?

She strikes a match and lowers it to the lamp. A certain brightness springs to life, overtakes the dark room. She sinks to her chair, puts her feet on the hassock. John is out there she knows, out in the jungle sleeping peacefully she hopes, unaware of her own day's toil, of her heartache.

In America there is a man named Mark Twain who will see Alice's photos of this most dreadful news from the Congo, will join with others in what will become known as the Congo Reform Society. But Alice has no thought other than rest as her head lowers, her glasses slipping down her slender nose. She dozes in her chair and doesn't know that tonight she will sleep deeply, the shadows moving westward, away from her.

Author's Note

On December 29th, 2003 I read a succinct account in *The Globe And Mail* of this remarkable woman named Alice Seeley Harris. The journalist who wrote it was Stephanie Nolan. I wrote to thank her for bringing Alice to my attention.

What is happenstance in our lives and what is planned ahead for us? I have asked myself that question many times since reading Ms. Nolan's article because it has changed the way I think. That is the power of good writing.

I contacted Dr. Jack Thompson of the University of Edinburgh's Center for The Study of Christianity in the Non-Western World. Dr. Thompson was kind enough to send me a journal that included Alice's photo. I thank him for providing me with a visual key to Alice. I see the firm jawline of a woman who wouldn't be afraid, who would plod on with true British resolve.

I have also been in touch with Anti-Slavery International in England and have discovered that Alice's lantern slides are stored "in two dusty wooden boxes on the ground floor of a small, low-rent building in south London."

I have taken fictional license with her story. I don't know who gave Alice her camera, but I do understand it was a gift before she sailed off with Mr. Harris. I like to think it was from her parents, in a moment of forgiveness and largesse. What I have done here is to preserve truth and that is all that counts in the final analysis. Truth must prevail. Alice knew that.

Like Alice, I too am intrigued by the power of light to erase darkness. I have entitled my story "Noon–Day Bright". It is a phrase from a Victorian missionary hymn entitled "We've A Story To Tell To The Nations," written by Ernest Nichol in 1896. That title was Alice's credo. She did have a story to tell the Congolese but she had no idea that they had a story to tell her. "Noon-Day Bright" refers to the joyful light that enters the world when we are exposed to truth.

Alice believed in her message but she was eager to accept the lessons that the Congolese had to teach *her*. When we view ourselves as *teacher*, we often need to become *learner*. It is only then that the cycle of human relationships be made whole, that the cycle of giving and receiving comes to fruition. That cycle puts a stop to one-upmanship and Imperialism.

Alice's legacy was her desire to effect social change. It was through her clear-minded focus and fortitude that the world was alerted to the dreadful abuses of human life in Leopold's Congo.

It was Alice who brought down a Kingdom with her Kodak photos.

From what I can discover at this point, it appears to be her husband, John Hobbis Harris, who was hailed with great regard in all of the textbooks on early Congo missionary work and reform. His papers and books are archived at Oxford University in the Bodleian Library. The Monarch bestowed a Knighthood, making him known hence as Sir John Hobbis Harris. Alice thus became Lady Alice on the strength of her husband's accomplishments and honours, rather than for her own work.

It appears that there are no extant letters either *from* or *to* Lady Alice that I am able to uncover at the time of writing. I am presently in correspondence with her great-granddaughter and her grandson, both of whom live in Britain.

Information is scarce.

Alice is rarely mentioned.

MRS. HOLLAND

Jean Ryan

I SIT HERE ON THIS FINE AFTERNOON with a pot of tea, gazing out the window of my new home.

Although I am not much prone to introspection, the occurrences of the last few years, in truth of the last several months, have been of such import that I feel the need to collect my thoughts. As I have rarely expressed those thoughts aloud, I have deduced that the best manner in which to proceed will be via pen. Writing has always been a source of comfort to me, and so I will begin. But where shall I start? I shall begin at the beginning.

In truth, I do not recall the first time I saw him, but do have hazy memories of a rather nice young man. We would have met in Dublin, as his parents were great friends of my mother's family. It was in London that he first made an impression on me. Mr. Wilde was lecturing and I pressed my brother into service as my companion. I was captivated by the gentleman's delivery as well as his subject matter. He was articulate and witty, clever with words. We spoke with him after the programme had concluded and he was quite charming.

It was not long thereafter that my brother and I were invited to call on Mrs. Wilde for tea.

Oscar was quite attentive and we passed a pleasant afternoon. Although we saw each other on occasion, I had no clear sense of his intentions, or if indeed he had any intentions at all. My family expressed some concern, as there had been unflattering references to him in the popular papers.

Given my previous broken engagement, I had not allowed myself to daydream in the manner of a young girl. I was prepared to wait and merely enjoy the pleasure of his company. I had, after all, the gratification of my books and my piano and had no difficulty in passing the time.

~

What I can recall with great clarity is how elated I was when Oscar did propose. He was so popular by then and in demand. He dressed himself with flair and expressed such marvelous opinions, that I was quite bemused at the thought that he would see in me something of great worth. He queried me on all manner of subjects and expressed delight in my rather unconventional views. He told me often in those days that my mind held great attraction for him – my liberal viewpoint especially. Of course, having known his mother, it was not surprising to me to find that he appreciated women who were passionate and independent thinkers.

~

The first years of our marriage were truly blissful. The only shadow cast was due to Oscar's insistence that our home be decorated to his exacting standards and designs, which resulted in our having to take rooms for a number of months while workmen laboured day and night in hopes they could please him.

I must stop now, as it is time for dinner.

~

It has been several days since I have written anything. I have just come in from a walk in the clear Swiss air. In addition to relief from the stares of neighbours and strangers and the pressures all around me, I am hoping that the move to this lovely land will benefit my health. My primary motive, of course, has been the welfare of my sons. My sons! My poor innocent sons! I could not chance their being subjected to the ridicule and bullying that seems so often to be great sport among schoolboys. Their father's public pillorying, as well as lurid reports of the trial, have been topics of great interest, both in press and parlour alike.

Upon landing, we assumed an old name from my family and I believe that the people here understand me to be recently widowed. I have not deliberately misled anyone, but rather have framed my responses in such a way as to deflect additional comment. Perhaps they noted my somber attire and distress upon our arrival, and attributed them to mourning. Little did they realize that I had made every attempt not to call attention to my sons or to myself as we fled England.

Although I continue to have some stiffness in my lower limbs, I remain hopeful that the fresh Alpine air will rejuvenate me. My family refers to my delicate constitution, but I do not think of myself as delicate, but rather slight of build, and suffering from the tribulations of the recent times.

In any case, I must resume my story. I remain steadfast in my belief that Oscar loved me when we were wed – well and truly loved me. We spent many blissful hours discussing literature and the theatre, as well as politics and women's suffrage. When Cyril was born, Oscar was ecstatic. He was proud and in awe of this marvelous creature we had produced. He praised the child to all who would listen and spent endless hours with him.

I now believe that it was when I was growing large with Vyvyan that the actual change occurred. I was told I was glowing, as expectant women are said to do, and that I looked more womanly. Perhaps that is what repulsed Oscar. Or it may be that he merely lost interest and was ready to move on to the next pursuit. I am not sure that even he himself could explain what happened. Although the initial shock has passed, I find I am not able to give consideration to his subsequent misadventures. History will no doubt provide more than ample record of the error of his ways, and I can only hope that his accomplishments and genius are recorded as well.

My family has been pressing me to divorce him, but that I will not do. I made a vow that was meant to last a lifetime and I intend to honour it despite whatever forces seem to work against me. Perhaps it is his true nature that has emerged, and his passion for me was merely a passing fancy, but I know that he loved me at one time and that his love for his sons endures.

I have suffered many hours of self-doubt and blame. I considered, at one point, that I should have attended more to my dress. I have never been particularly interested in the fashion of the day, but Oscar was always noticing the smallest details of a person's toilet. Indeed, he designed my wedding gown and those of my bridesmaids. When we moved into our perfect home, he insisted that I dress in a fashion which reflected the room in which we would be entertaining. I complied in order to please him, as I felt it my wifely duty, but I suffered through every moment. I felt more like an organ grinder's monkey than a hostess, and could only imagine what our guests were thinking.

In those times as well, I believed I was too quiet and think now that if I had been more flamboyant, like Lillie Langtree or Sarah Bernhardt, perhaps our lives would have ended differently. But I have more recently been assured that he did not have any amorous relations with these women, and so it seems that any changes in my behavior might have, at best, only delayed the inevitable.

The boys will do well I am sure, as they are both quite bright and have exquisite manners. They will no doubt learn of their father's difficulties, but for now, have only been told that there have been serious troubles and that it is best for us to bide a while in Switzerland. Being obedient and well-bred, they have not asked anything more of me, and seem to have adapted to their new school with no difficulty. Oh, to have the resilience of the young!

Today I find myself scanning the heavens as if the skies will open and an angel will descend to guide me. Should that occur, I would ask what will become of me. I am fortunate to have received the Marriage Settlement from my grandfather, so I am able to live in a reasonable manner. I have no desire to enter into society here, so my expenses will be scant. Perhaps after a suitable period, I will visit friends of my family in Italy. I am trusting that their love of my grandparents will cause them to welcome "Mrs. Holland" with open arms and few questions.

Author's Note

Oscar Wilde's plays continue to be performed today. Many people know of the scandal of his homosexual liaison with Alfred "Bosie" Douglas and his subsequent trial and imprisonment, but I have met few who were aware that prior to that he was married and fathered two sons.

Constance Lloyd was an accomplished woman in her own right and I believe that Wilde loved her and his sons throughout his life.

OLIVE BRANCHES AND ARROWS

Todd McKinstry

She sat on the edge of the Lincoln bed rearranging the sheets and blankets, as she had so many other things, into a more comfortable reality. Plump little fingers tugged, pulled and straightened as she talked in a soft voice, her eyes slightly diverted from her husband in bed, half upright, slouching to one side.

She stood up and walked to the window and looked out towards the magnolia and cherry trees on the sweeping west lawn. She heard the sound of the sheep as they grazed there and she smiled and thought proudly of the wool they'd auctioned off for the war effort. After all of the heatless and meatless days they'd endured in the residence to set an example, the war was over.

"Mr. Lansing has had a series of cabinet meetings," she said as she let out a long protracted breath. "I know, I know. Disappointing. He did it completely without your authority."

She sat in a chair by the window, drew a pad of paper across the table towards her and began to make notes. On the table beside her were similar pads filled with indecipherable script.

"I should think it is high time for Mr. Lansing to go. He's had his day. He can't do any more for the Treaty in any regard and you should, at least, be served by somebody who is loyal. I'd thought of Bainbridge Colby as a replacement for him as Secretary of State." She sat back in the chair, her eyes averted from the bed yet still cognizant of the low rasping breaths punctuated by muted coughs.

"I agree," she said as she continued to write. "Vice-President Marshall's requests to see you are simply out of the question. Completely." She went on making notes, lifting her head slightly for the responses to her queries and considerations that never came. "I've been clear that you oughtn't be bothered with anything but the most crucial affairs. It being my stewardship," she added, pausing to savour the last word, "I'll give them ample and detailed notes of your responses to any of their concerns."

She set the pen down on the table, stood up and circled the bed, then drew the blanket around her husband's shoulders as he stared at her with a half smile, a little spittle trickling down his chin which she daubed at with a handkerchief. "Senator Fall insists on checking on your health and this, I think, since he is a representative of the Senate this will have to be arranged." She stood back and examined the figure of her husband in the bed and her cheeks puffed out a little and her lips pursed. "In a couple of weeks."

She forced a smile and left the room, closing the door firmly behind her as an usher stood up from his chair and nodded.

"Nobody but the doctors or myself are allowed in until I give further notice," she said as she turned and strode briskly down the corridor.

"Yes, ma'am," the usher replied as he sat back down and unfolded the newspaper he'd been reading. The front page told the story of the President's temporary exhaustion and his need for extensive rest. His European trip to make the peace had taken its toll and now there was a desperate effort to ratify the Treaty that would create the League of Nations but those efforts seemed stalled in the Senate.

The usher's eyes wandered away from his newspaper to the closed door beside him and he stared for a moment then shook his head from side to side.

She went downstairs, then outside through the Rose Garden past the twisted limbs of the Jackson Magnolia to the Oval Office where a Secretary was waiting for her.

"Good morning, ma'am," the secretary said with a half smile.

"Good morning." She crossed the floor and stood by the desk in front of the window. It was a gift from Queen Victoria fashioned out of timbers that had once been the HMS Resolute, now quite literally the seat of power. She pondered the seat behind the desk, then stopped and went to sit on the settee in the corner.

The secretary brought over a stack of papers and set them on an adjacent table. "Correspondence and pressing questions from the Cabinet and Congress ma'am."

"And they'll all be answered."

"Senator Hitchcock is here as well. You had arranged an appointment with him."

'Fine," she said as she leafed through the pile of papers. "Send him in."

The secretary opened the door and an elegant man in a blue pin-striped suit strode in, hat in hand.

"Good morning Mrs. Wilson," he said.

"Senator," she replied as she pored over the papers in front of her, black horn-rimmed glasses perched precariously on the end of her nose.

"The President is well?"

"Recovering. The doctors insist on extensive rest as you are well aware."

"I understand, Mrs. Wilson." He walked towards the window and stared outside. "As liaison to the President I imagine you are aware the Treaty, as it is now framed, will not pass the Senate."

She looked up, slid her glasses off and glared.

"I have a list of certain accommodations and amendments which would insure the likelihood of the Treaty passing a vote in the Senate."

"Absolutely not. The President is adamant that the Treaty must be passed as is."

"But ma'am ..." he said as his voice trailed off. "Simply put, the Treaty, as is, will not pass."

"Come, come, Senator. That's you job, is it not? To get things done." She looked up again with arched eyebrows.

He took a deep breath. "The President does understand?"

She stood up with her hands planted on her hips. "Of course the President understands and I believe I've made his views clear to you, have I not"

"Of course madam, I understand." He watched as she moved across the room, her feet moving casually over the carpeted image of an eagle, one set of talons with olive branches, the other with arrows.

"I could use the assistance of Mr. Grey however. The British have sent him to assist in the passage of the Treaty."

"Mr. Grey?" she asked. "Do I know a Mr. Grey?"

"The British representative, ma'am. You haven't ... I mean the President hasn't accepted his credentials as of yet."

"No, I don't believe that he has, has he? I must really look into that," she said as the gaunt, bearded image of a man looked out from a painted portrait on the wall behind her.

Pleasantries were exchanged and Hitchcock left and met his aid in the hall as he listened to the door shut firmly behind him.

"Any luck?" the aid asked.

"None at all."

"We're dead in the water then."

"Yes, I believe that we are."

"And for what?"

Hitchcock shook his head. "And she's not even going to accept Grey's credentials either."

"Good God, why not?"

"For some silly joke Grey's aid has been telling at cocktail parties. That's why not."

"Joke?"

"You haven't heard?"

The aid shrugged his shoulders.

Hitchcock let out a breath. "The joke is what did Mrs. Galt do when the President proposed marriage?"

The aid just stared and shook his head.

"She fell out of bed."

"My God, you're kidding me. That's why she won't accept Grey's credentials. Because some aid has been telling that joke about her?"

"And he's demoted the poor fellow as well and still, nothing. Grey was key in mobilizing support for this Treaty. Without him and with no apparent compromise … "

"It's like a damned regency." the aid said.

"And all by a woman who, five years ago, couldn't have named all the states let alone the branches of government. My God, she doesn't even believe in the right of women to vote. If the Nineteenth Amendment passes I can't imagine what the response will be … " He paused and spat out the final words, " … of this President."

Author's Note

More often than not, a more interesting rendering of history comes through a study of its footnotes and asterisks. One can read the accounts of Woodrow Wilson's Presidency and his lofty ideals until one discovers, unbeknownst to most Americans, he was incapacitated by a severe stroke for the last eighteen months of his final term in office. The Vice President never took over, even temporarily, and senior government officials and Cabinet members were kept largely in the dark. The only access they had to Wilson was through his wife, Edith. Interestingly, this event never seems to loom large in any history of Wilson's tenure and Edith Wilson appears as little more than a footnote in that drama.

During this period the Treaty of Versailles was defeated by the United States Senate, which effectively blocked any American participation in the newly formed League of Nations. The League was Wilson's own creation and it was his hope the institution would work to prevent another calamity like the Great War that had just ended. Furthermore, he feared that without it, the world would easily descend into a similar catastrophe, which indeed it did just twenty years later. Lofty ideals aside, Wilson's own intransigence, his refusal to compromise with the Republicans in the Senate led by Henry Cabot Lodge, is often cited as a major reason for the Treaty's failure.

The problem in trying to decide what actually happened is that we can't be sure who was making the decisions, Edith or Woodrow, and if it was Woodrow, what exactly was his mental state. The job of an historian is never to fictionalize, but one feels a certain license, knowing full well that the principal actors in this life drama worked so diligently to obscure or hide the truth.

"Olive Branches and Arrows" is a fictional look at a unique moment in American history and at one of the more interesting characters in that historical drama. In the end, such fiction draws on what facts we do have in order to generate interest in the people and events that seemed to have escaped the front pages of history, the footnotes and asterisks, many of whom are women, like Edith Bolling Wilson.

ANNIE TAYLOR

Carol Leigh Wehking

Annie Taylor sits in the sun, a lazy cat dozing on her lap. The year is 1920, and Annie is 82 years old. She is blind now, and her once lithe, strong body is shrunken with age and defeat. She is not sitting in a rocking chair in a parlour, a neglected extra auntie. She sits on the steps of the International Hotel in Niagara Falls, New York. Across the street is the river. Across the river is Canada, and the very rock upon which she stepped, the moment she made forgotten history.

Annie has a handful of postcards to sell, and a tin cup for the money. If you didn't know her story, you wouldn't give her a passing glance. You cannot read her history in her face; you cannot see the stoutness of her heart. You cannot measure her courage by the aged droop of her shoulders nor by the fumbling dim-sighted way she stumbles through her days.

You might have remembered her if you could see her in that plumed hat she wore in 1901 for the newspaper pictures, but that hat is long gone.

Inside the grey head, behind the blurred eyes, her own story of inspiration, of loss and courage, of despair and hope, of danger and redemption, transformation, disillusion, and betrayal plays over and over.

The seed was planted when Annie was a child of seven, travelling with her father. Her sisters preferred to stay at home, but she was always adventuresome, always ready for something outdoors with her brothers, something to challenge her wits and her body. She was small and muscular, a round-faced child with bright eyes, a defiantly jutting chin, and two fat brown braids that never stayed tidy. She sat beside her father on the wagon seat, straight and still.

It was a long ride to Niagara Falls, but she didn't really like travelling in the wagon. It was too noisy. At home in Auburn, she was accustomed to walking, and she could walk through the woods or the long grass as silently as on a dusty path. But the wagon creaked, and the harness squeaked, and the wheels jolted and rattled, and the horses snorted and snuffled, their hooves clopping on the hardpan: it was altogether too much noise for her liking. Too much noise to hear the whirr of insects or the song of birds, or even the music in her own head. And because she was trying so hard to hear at least that, she didn't hear the distant roar until she saw its evidence on the skyline.

She thought at first that it was smoke, but it was too white, too translucent, too diffuse. Maybe it was a sign of God. Maybe it was an angel! She was struck with wonder. Her father pulled the reins short, and the creaking and groaning of the wagon, the harness, the horses, all came to a stop. And as they gazed, and the noise they made fell still, they became aware of the roar. No one ever calls that noise anything else. The roar of the water. The plume of mist rising above it. A roaring angel.

They stared, not speaking. But then her father lifted the reins and shook them, and the horses tossed their heads, the creaking and clamour began again.

"Stop!" she cried, and her father reined in in alarm. She scrambled down from the wagon and called back up to him that she would walk behind, that he should move on without her.

He looked hard at her, but then without a word, he clucked to the team and the wagon moved away. She stood still until the roar of the water engulfed and then overwhelmed the sound of harness, horses, and wagon, and all she could hear was the water. Keeping her eyes on the angel plume, she moved slowly toward it, moving into the sound of it until she felt that she was alone in the world, surrounded by an unknown reverberation that erased the landscape, the other sounds, even the smells. The river rushed by at her side, drawing her along with it, into the heart of the angel who bellowed an irresistible call. Other travellers may have passed her, but once her father was out of sight, she gave herself over to the sight and sound that swallowed up her senses.

When at last she actually reached the rim of Niagara Falls, the vastness of the water surging over the edge and plunging into the deep tumbled spray below drew her as if her blood and this heavy rush of water were of the same stream. At last her waiting father lifted her back into the wagon. If he had not, she would never have turned away of her own accord.

And like the river that does not know it will tumble over a great escarpment, and plummet crashing to the rocks below, her life flowed forward: she grew up, went to Normal School, got married ... not knowing that her husband would die and that she would find herself alone in the world with no one to love, and no means of support – dashed to pieces on the rocks of his death.

It was all she could do to gather her courage about her and take on her own life. She travelled here and there, taught school, attempted to find a place for herself, and an income to augment her inheritance so that she might live with the comforts she was used to having. Even with a college degree and the ability to teach French and Spanish and instrumental music, she found no work to keep her.

At last she trained to become a dance instructor, and landed in Bay City, Michigan, a lumber town far from her origins. She started a dancing school in the lumber town. It began well enough, but as the town's fortunes declined, so did the school's. And when that, too, left her bereft, she pulled together the tatters of her life and conceived a plan so bold and desperate that some would call her crazy. If life were to be so full of hidden rocks upon which to founder, she would seek out real ones, and challenge them with all she had left: her real body and her own spirit. She was drawn back to the river that cascaded unceasingly over the escarpment of Niagara. To that place she set her course, offering herself into the arms of the roar which had called her back over all the years, called her into its arms.

The plan was her design from start to finish: she had a barrel made under her direction, from a pattern shaped upon her own silhouette. The cooper's sister – and the townspeople as well – looked upon the endeavour with contempt: what could a proper lady be doing, even to contemplate such an unseemly adventure? But Annie pressed onward against the disapproval, the outright criticism, and gave her life over to the deed ahead.

And now Annie nods in the sun. Her world has dimmed: she doesn't know who passes her, who pauses, who smiles or who mocks. She answers when she thinks someone speaks. Sometimes she is not sure whether someone really speaks, or whether she is in a dream. Did a woman really stop and bend and speak her name?

"Annie Taylor. You changed my life," said the voice beside her ear.

In that short journey over the abyss, she had found herself, her life, her aliveness, her infinity, her invulnerability. But this was not what the sneering, peering public wished to know. They wanted to hear about the icy water, the ghastly nothingness of the fall, the lack of air, the first breath after the lid was hacked off, the bruises. Her heroic moment was over; the instant of understanding and completeness, the revelation, the enlightenment, the moment of truth, over in a heartbeat. Now all that was left was her story, a story no one wanted to hear.

Yet a woman is bending down to her with respect, even awe. Is this a dream?

Annie listens, as the voice, who calls herself Caroline, goes on to tell her own story: she had been a lady of the night when Annie first came to Niagara Falls with her barrel and her bravery. There were pictures in the paper, and Caroline had recognized the hat. She had seen Annie, a small, plain woman past her prime, and she marveled that this was the creature who sealed herself into a wooden chamber of her own design, and went over the precipice of her own will.

"I am alive," Annie Taylor had said to the crowds and the reporters, and to herself. Caroline had gazed at the headlines at the newsstand. This woman Annie Taylor had done this thing, this death-defying stunt as some called it. She had defied something, no doubt. Caroline could think of nothing bigger, more powerful, or more frightening than the falls, the rapids, the whirlpool, which had claimed the lives of so many others. Yet this greying woman had challenged that power, and come out alive. Caroline had stared long at the photographs. Just a short defiant old woman wearing a well-made hat.

No hat at all coming out of the barrel.

Caroline's story went on and on. Annie wasn't sure whether she was listening or dreaming.

"And so I thought, if she can brave the Falls, and pull herself alive out of the barrel, from the churn of rock and water, I can pull myself out of this life I'm leading. It was the hat that gave me the idea. I've been a milliner these seventeen years, and every feather I sew onto a hat, I think of you. Come," said the voice of Caroline gently, "let me buy you a cup of coffee. Come with me," she urged, trying to pull Annie up by the elbow. But Annie shook off the hand, shook off the dream.

A milliner, a maker of feathered hats. Dimly Annie could remember choosing that upright white plume on her own hat, because it was like the angel plume of spray above the falls.

On the day of the event, she had never thought of turning back. Never let her mind scramble to safety and give up the whole idea. By that time, she had gone beyond choice or repentance. She clambered inside the barrel, cringed briefly as the lid was pounded into place, tried to discipline her breathing as air was pumped in. And then the barrel was cast over the back of the rowboat, and towed bouncing and scraping into the current, there cut loose. Had she screamed to be pulled ashore, she could not have made herself heard. But she did not scream.

She had been alone in the world, inside her barrel. She had not known whether it was to be a ship or a coffin. Would she sail to salvation, or go under the pounding cataract and there make her end? It had been an eternity there in the darkness and thunder, an eternity in which the difference between life and death had ceased to be significant. A timeless age in which the reasons for doing anything had been drowned out by the heave and buffet of water against oak. During which inward and outward strength battled each other until both were victorious. So often she wished she had done the thing without the barrel.

She is alone in the world now, without her barrel, in the darkness; in the heave and buffet of life around her, no one would ever know, no matter what she said or how she said it, what had really happened for her when she entered her oaken vessel and challenged Niagara Falls. She had not conquered the Falls. She had been *accepted by* them. She had entered their domain. She had earned their companionship. From inside her barrel, her life was taken over by that pounding, trembling, roaring. Her roaring angel. In whose arms she had once been brutally cradled. Into whose arms she now willingly withdrew.

Author's Notes

I can't remember how Annie Taylor first came to my attention: perhaps when I took my children to the Daredevil museum at Niagara Falls one March Break. Later, as a storyteller seeking women subjects, I took an interest in the interior lives of some whose external accomplishments are their chief heritage. After reading Joan Murray's remarkable book-length poem, *Queen of the Mist,* I knew I had to discover Annie Taylor from the inside, and originally wrote the story in the first person. However, when it came time to tell it with my storytelling group, Uppity Women, it seemed that third person was more appropriate, and so that is how it came to be. I have told the story of Annie Taylor at festivals, concerts, and schools, and have always found my audience as captivated with her as I am.

Regarding the real Annie Taylor:

Annie Taylor was not the first person to think of going over Niagara Falls in some sort of vessel, but she is the first to have done it. She grew up Anna Edson, daughter of a prosperous mill-owning family in Auburn, New York (where Harriet Tubman, another of my heroes, also had a home). Her father died when she was 12, but left the family well provided for. After Normal School where she trained to be a teacher, she married David Taylor when she was just 17 years old. They had a son, but the child died when only a few days old. Annie was 25 when David was killed in the Civil War. She had some inheritance from her family, but not enough to maintain her taste for good things, and she traveled far in search of some manner of keeping herself before she ended in Bay City, Michigan, with her dancing school for young ladies. (I have found no record of her teaching otherwise).

She was in need of something momentous to save her, when she hit upon the idea of the Niagara Falls adventure. She contracted Franklin ("Tussie") Russell, a sideshow promoter, to back the project. Annie really did design her barrel, shaped roughly as she was, narrow at the legs, larger in the middle, smaller at the top for her head. It was padded with a mattress and pillows and had an anvil attached to the bottom. It was not as tall as she was, and weighed the same. She had been rowed into the river with the barrel, wearing proper Victorian dress, but she discreetly changed behind the shrubbery of Little Grass Island into a *slightly* more practical costume before entering the barrel. A bicycle pump was used to add air, and then the barrel was towed into the river and released. It drifted rapidly to the Canadian side to pitch over Horseshoe Falls. She spent, in all, less than an hour and a half in the barrel, but it took only seventeen minutes from being cut loose from the boat that towed her into the river, to get to the bottom of the falls. It was another twenty minutes or so before the barrel could be hooked ashore on the Canadian side of the river, with another hiatus before they could get the lid cut off and release her.

She said at the time that she was in her 40s, but evidence suggests she was 63 when she went over the falls on her birthday, October 24, 1901. Annie hoped that this unheard-of stunt would be the making of her fortune: that she would become famous and go on a lecture tour that would pay her handsomely. This never came to pass. Her tour was with a sideshow, rather tawdry, certainly not erudite or philosophical. She was neither young nor glamorous nor male, and therefore of little interest to sideshow audiences; they sought thrills, not a story of internal transformation. Her barrel was displayed with her until it was eventually stolen. She actually did the lecture circuit for a short time, but was swindled by a succession of managers and eventually ended up back in Niagara Falls selling penny postcards and living in an almshouse in Lockport, N.Y., where she died on April 29, 1921.

Another wry note is that an Englishman, Bobby Leach, seemed to be a fan of hers for a time – followed her about asking all manner of questions. In reality, he was picking her brains for ideas for a similar stunt: ten years after Annie's trip, Bobby went over the falls in a similarly designed barrel, but made of metal. He was much better at self-promotion, and did reasonably well selling himself and his story, but died of gangrene in New Zealand a few years later.

My chief influence in writing this story is Joan Murray's *Queen of the Mist*, published by Beacon Press in 1999. Murray painted the interior landscape beautifully, fully supported by research. Unable to get my hands on Annie's own memoirs, I amalgamated the available information for background facts, then "went inside" and found my Annie there.

SYRIE

Lise Lévesque

THE DRESSING TABLE STOOD OUT LIKE A deformed albino amid a shipment of English country furniture being unloaded at Sotheby's Gallery. A seven-drawer affair supported by cabriole legs and redone in white by some trend-setting iconoclast, it appeared to be a faux Louis Quinze. Stewart Hunter sighed. Ever since the Wall Street Crash of 1929, English aristocrats had been dropping off horrors on auctioneers who were at a loss as to how to dispose of them. Everyone it seemed was trying to liquidate their assets.

Upon inspection, the albino surrendered a small ledger from its velvet-lined jewelery drawer. It showed former sales of mirrors, statuettes and Regency chairs. Hunter wondered if its proprietor – one Gwendolyn Syrie Wellcome Maugham – had left the book in the vanity on purpose. Or had it been an oversight? Hoping that the ledger would help with other evaluations, he locked it back in the compartment, pocketed the key and left in search of a matching mirror. As he went about the business of checking armoires and tables against the manifest, his mind kept drifting back to the owner of his find. *Wellcome-Maugham.* The name sounded familiar. *There is a writer called Maugham. Somerset Maugham. Of course ... the author of "The Circle," that facetious play about marriage. This must be his ... This desk must belong to his wife.*

Hunter remembered Syrie's photograph from the Society pages. A thin-lipped woman with a generous nose, dark hair and eyes, posing with stylish confidence. *If my memory serves me, she was – must still be, the poor dear – in the decorating business. A tad vulgar, those coral interiors featuring palm tree torcheres, but ...*

Too distracted for serious cataloguing, he returned to the mysterious ledger. On its back pages, he saw drawings for tall niches in stairwells, measurements for panels to be covered in antique wallpaper – one outrageous sketch after another. Each page was adding to his amusement, until he stumbled upon the draft of a letter. Almost illegible – so many words had been crossed out of the document – yet, far too intriguing and salacious to be left undeciphered. Hunter took the find to his office, lit himself a pipe and resumed his reading.

Mon Cher Maurice,

As you must know by now, my beloved William has taken up permanent residence at la Villa Mauresque. So, it shouldn't come as a surprise to you that, at this juncture, I feel so dejected as to file for a divorce. He knows that except for yearly visits, this arrangement will rob Liza of a father. Yet, he has made clear to us that he prefers living in France with the unsavoury Haxton to sharing day-to-day life with his wife and child.

Forgive me for being so abrupt in dropping my concerns in your lap but I am in urgent need of legal advice. The time has come for sentiments to be put aside so that I can protect my daughter's interests as well as my own. Given the circumstances, however, I find myself in a quandary. To seek a divorce on grounds of adultery seems in order.

Yet, I have been told that under the Criminal Law Amendment Act of 1885, it might be folly to undertake such an action in England. In fact, it could bring upon my husband a fate similar to that of Oscar Wilde – a two-year sentence for consorting with a man. As furious as I feel towards Willie, I have to bear in mind his relationship to Liza. So, I would appreciate your opinion as to whether the Napoleonic Code would be kinder to him. Then, to further complicate matters, we were wed in America, he resides in France and I live here. So, what am I to do? Hire an English Solicitor, or start proceedings under your expertise?

The darling argues that I was cognizant of his penchant before I married him, and furthermore, that I blackmailed him into marriage. At that, I am appalled. You belonged to his circle of friends at the time William and I met, Maurice. If you recall, he had been madly in love with that actress Sue Jones. So, not only did I think him capable of loving a woman, I assumed that he understood our vows to be a shared commitment to monogamy. I was wrong.

Now, he claims that we had agreed on a quiet, platonic way of life – one that would support his writing – in exchange for his giving me a child. In retrospect, I believe that William used my friendship – something I valued as the basis for a growing intimacy. It seems to me that once I was pregnant with Liza, he offered to assume his responsibilities because it created a convenient smokescreen for his relationship with Haxton. I realized it too late and I found myself trapped. Not only was the rejection excruciating, I have had to weather loneliness and keep up a front, for years, so that the man I had grown to love would not be subjected to discrimination and imprisonment.

I do not mean to imply innocence or naivety on my part during our courtship. After all, I was still legally bound to Henry Wellcome, my elder by twenty-six years. You probably aren't aware that that dreadful union, imposed on me by my father, had produced a mentally retarded son whom Henry quickly farmed out to a foster home. To meet the captivating Somerset Maugham brightened my world. To befriend him softened me up to the consistency of clay. By the time he proposed I was totally smitten. He could have moulded me into the person most apt to fulfill his needs, but unbeknownst to me, Haxton had already been cast in that role.

That ridiculous wedding ceremony in New Jersey was an omen of humiliations to come. There we stood, in front of a Justice of the Peace, surrounded by drunks awaiting sentencing. That was in 1917. With war upon us and bombs falling over our heads, what did William do? He curtailed our honeymoon, signed up with Intelligence Services and got himself sent to work as a go-between in Russia. That little adventure got him stranded in a sanatorium with a bout of tuberculosis. My only hope was that he would use the time to reflect. I was still in awe of him, as were his many followers in those days. Gerald Kelly himself, drew one portrait after another of the prolific Willie. I should have paid more heed to the one entitled "The Jester." In hindsight I realize that it summed up all the dandyish arrogance I had ignored.

So little of our life resembled the façade we put up for our friends. Finally I had to branch out and cultivate some relationships of my own. I wanted to earn a living. Women depend on men because society propagates this state of affairs, but we do need and like our independence. So, I transformed my life by transforming dull English dwellings. I was hailed for my white-on-white interiors; the first to turn decorating into an art form; appreciated by the likes of Mrs. Simpson and the Prince of Wales. The more I made a name for myself as a decorator, however, the more he berated my work. William has a sharp tongue for a man who stammers.

Try living with someone who demands your attention while he hammers words like 'propinquity' at you. To offset his communication problems, he creates characters who transparently depict the people he wishes to ridicule. It was me and my work he derided when he wrote that Mrs. Tower in "Jane" was "seized with a prevailing passion for decorating. Everything that could be pickled was pickled," he said, "and what couldn't be pickled was painted." Once, he told our guests at a diner party: "Hold tight to your chairs. They are certainly for sale." He was angry, I admit, because I had sold his desk without asking. As a thing of beauty and the cherished possession of a recognized writer, it caught the eye of the Duchess of Portarlington. I had intended to make good for it, but he looked upon the transaction as a declaration of war.

As to that rough cut, liar and gambler, Gerald Haxton, what can I say? While posing as William's secretary, he has usurped my role as a wife. It humiliates me but Willie claims to need him as a travelling mate because of his talent for separating the bores from the wits. And so, while I struggle, they have their adventures. In 1919, they spent six months in the East together. Having sailed from Saigon to Shanghai, they journeyed on the Yangtze River for 1500 miles, then walked all the way to the walled city of Chung King. Upon his return, he dedicated his travel book, "On Chinese Screen" to me. How tactful of my husband to offer me a permanent reminder of those nights, when he and Gerald were holding each other's gaze, under the sampans' lanterns. Though he is known for his Edwardian manners, he can be a small man in more than stature at times!

These days, he would like me to fade into oblivion. "Don't make scenes," he insists, as he did before abandoning Liza and me in London during the war. I try to keep face but isolation and despair weigh me down. No matter how tall I stand on the sandbar of my failed marriage to Monsieur Somerset Maugham, each new tide of gossip engulfs me in greater depths of social disgrace. That failure, born of his need for "decency" and suckled at the empty breast of convenience, will be worn by me alone. Women lose face to divorce; men acquire sympathy.

With luck, he'll leave us with a roof over our heads. King Road, perhaps? In all candour, the Rolls and a chauffeur would help. As you see, Maurice, I am modest in my wants and eager to avoid scandal. The man wishes to be free and so he shall be. Trusting you will be discreet in legal searches and kind with advice, I await your answer.

With gratitude,
Syrie

Stewart Hunter took off his glasses, sat back and refilled his pipe. Moved by the poignancy of Syrie's letter, he faced a quandary of his own. According to the manifest, neither the ledger nor its enclosed letter had been registered as separate items from the dressing table. Outside of Mrs. Maugham whose act of forgetfulness was questionable, only he knew of their existence. The Gallery had a reputation to uphold and he could not be careless in disseminating information. Yet, he wondered what he should do? *I could return the ledger but what if I embarrass her? On the other hand, a generous amount of pounds Sterling could probably be had from Maugham himself for this document.*

Feeling wicked and powerful, Hunter pocketed both the book and its precious enclosure. As the day wore on, he found himself considering a third option. Somerset Maugham may have had a way with words but his scorned wife knew how to express feelings, as well. Her side of the story deserved to be heard. He could wait a while, then look for a private collector … per chance, one whose generosity was accompanied by an appetite for gossip. Now that was tempting ...

Author's Note

When I heard of Bernadette Rule's intention to collect fictitious stories of women connected to famous men, the feminist in me rose to the occasion. I had just purchased tickets for "The Circle," at the 2007 Shaw Festival. I knew the play to be an exposé of married life by the infamous Somerset Maugham and began to ponder his wife's feelings on the subject.

That meditation let me down a longer path than anticipated. So much has been written by and about the prolific 20th Century writer that I found myself reading for pleasure as well as devouring information from two biographical tomes. They were Ted Morgan's *Maugham - A Biography*, released by Simon and Schuster, New York in 1980 and Jeffrey Meyers' *Somerset Maugham - A Life*, published by Alfred. A. Knopf, New York in 2004. To add to my delight, these horns of plenty were replete with photographs of the Maughams themselves, their homes, families of origin and relations.

Also, I found a chronology of the writer's life – on a web site managed by members.shaw.ca – that had been framed in the world events of the era. Then, while perusing through *W. Somerset Maugham - The Complete Short Stories,* volumes one, two and three, I reread "A Marriage of Convenience" and the story "Rain", which was later made into one of the first talking films. Finally, I read *The Summing Up*, an autobiographical account written in 1938 and referring to what he hoped for in a marriage and *The Moon and Sixpence* which reflects the deterioration of William's relationship to Syrie.

Armed with all this information, I began to tremble at the idea of compressing it into a believable, yet fictitious short story, involving Gwendolyn Syrie Wellcome Maugham. However, an article on "Syrie, the Decorator" written by Robert Plunket in *Sarasota Magazine* 29.1, October 2006, gave me more insight into her personal deeds. It led me to research English auctioneers in the 1920s and, once I found the Sotheby's Gallery at www.answers.com, a story that could incorporate hers began to take form.

So, there you have the deconstruction of my short story, "Syrie." Having felt through its research that Mrs Maugham's life, views and feelings deserved to be known, I can only hope to have risen to the task.

THE SWAN SONG

William Chan

DARK CLOUDS KEPT ROLLING IN FROM THE NORTH all morning. By midday, thunder began to rumble in the distance. I looked out of the window and saw a pair of nasty crows fly by, squawking. It worried me that my husband had gone to work without his umbrella. But as rain started to come down, I heard the key turn in the door and Enrique rushed in, almost out of breath.

"Just made it!" he declared with a broad grin and embraced me.

We sat down to a plateful of our favourite tapas and Enrique poured out some Manzanilla. When our housekeeper Maria brought in the main course, the storm was raging with full force. All of a sudden, there was a knock on the door. Enrique and I looked at each other in amazement. Who could be visiting in such weather? Maria went to the door, came back and handed something to my husband.

"A telegram for you, dear." He passed it on to me.

"For me?" My hands were shaking. I nearly dropped the envelope as I was opening it.

"What does it say?" Enrique asked when I fell silent.

"It's from Manuela. Pilar died early this morning." I crossed myself.

"Oh, I am so sorry. You were such good friends at school. Wasn't it Pilar who married the musician?"

"Yes. The funeral is tomorrow. Manuela has asked me to stay with her in Barcelona tonight."

"Good. I will go with you to the station on my way back to work. The afternoon train should take you there before it gets dark."

"I hope you don't mind, Enrique. Maria will have your dinner ready."

While Enrique was having a siesta, I packed a black dress in my little suitcase. Then I slumped into the armchair, overwhelmed by memories of school days. We were such good friends – Manuela, Pilar and I. What were we like in those days? I found my photo album after a frantic search. There it was, the picture of our graduating class, badly faded now. How carefree we looked, the three of us sitting in the front row. Those were the best years of our lives! We all came from prominent families and Santa Teresa was clearly the finest school in Barcelona. With little effort, Pilar and Manuela excelled in math and literature while I was first in philosophy. Sharp-witted and confident, we were never at a loss for a clever argument. No wonder we were nicknamed *las chicas intrèpidas*, the fearless girls!

Pilar and I had a special bond as we were both so fond of music. She loved to play the piano whereas I was good with the violin. We enjoyed going to concerts and would sometimes play duets together. But more than anything, I remember Pilar for her fine taste in clothes. She would help Manuela and me pick the most elegant dresses and together we would stroll at a leisurely pace down Las Ramblas, the fashionable street where almost all of Barcelona would gather in the evening. What an impression we must have made! As I thought of Pilar and her stylish clothes, an extraordinary scene came flashing back to me.

It was just two months before graduation and the camellias were in full bloom. Everyone was excited about the future. Manuela had arranged to work with her uncle's law firm and I had been accepted by the nursing school in Valencia. Somehow Pilar seemed withdrawn and missed our evening stroll a couple of times. But we didn't think much of it until we got a mysterious invitation from her. To begin with, it said nothing about the occasion and then it wasn't going to be at her parents' house! Instead, the address was in a working-class district not known to any of us. We wanted to ask her more about it but she was nowhere to be found.

On the day of the party, we went upstairs to a tiny, poorly furnished apartment. We had brought wine and flowers and Pilar greeted us warmly but seemed preoccupied. Altogether seven or eight girls arrived and I realized that this was a gathering of her closest friends. Pilar served us sangria and we sat anxiously waiting to see what would happen. At last, she brought in a young man, introduced him as Carlos Casals and announced that they were going to get married! I knew right away he was her piano teacher but not everyone did. We were so stunned we didn't know what to say. When we recovered, we offered our congratulations and best wishes. Though we kissed her joyfully, she remained very solemn. She sat down next to Carlos and took his hand.

"My dear friends," she addressed us, "you have all been very kind. But I want you to know that from now on, my life will be completely different from what you and I have been accustomed to." She bit her lip and looked tenderly at Carlos.

"I have asked you to come here today," she continued, "to take away my expensive clothes. I won't need them anymore in my new life."

With that, she and Carlos brought out three large boxes full of the most elegant clothes and accessories. There was a magnificent dress in red silk embroidered with black lace that caught everyone's attention. It was too long for me but fitted Manuela perfectly. Pilar also had fine shoes of Italian calf leather that were exactly my size and some had never been worn. So Manuela and I received several of her most prized possessions. There was, however, something for each guest, be it a pair of gloves, a handbag, or just a mantilla. And when the boxes were finally empty, Pilar seemed somehow relieved. But we were shocked by what had happened and the room grew quiet. Luckily, I thought of something to break the awkward silence.

"Would Carlos perhaps play something for us?" I ventured, having spotted an old piano in the corner.

Carlos reddened quite visibly and made a faint gesture to decline. But Pilar smiled at him, and nodded firmly. There was no mistaking her wishes. And so he obliged and played. I was astonished by the exquisite sound that came out of the dilapidated instrument.

Pilar must have noticed my reaction, for she leaned towards me and whispered, "He tunes the piano himself everyday!"

The first piece was Debussy's "Claire de Lune" and this he played so delicately that one could almost sense the moonlight shimmering. In the candlelit room, the effect was simply magical. It was followed by two of Chopin's Nocturnes, which he interpreted with unusual tenderness. They were like serenades for Pilar who was beaming with pride. At that moment it was obvious that she was at peace with her decision, "for richer or for poorer". This was a scene from fifteen years ago, but I can picture it now as vividly as if it had happened yesterday.

At San Miguel station in Barcelona, Manuela was waiting for me with her carriage. She did not doubt for a moment that I would come. School friends were for life! We went to her parents' large mansion where she still lived, never having married. Her parents had hired an excellent cook and were able to put on a splendid dinner for me. The conversation was most congenial but I could see that Manuela was impatient to finish dinner and be left alone with me.

At last, having bid her parents good-night, I went up the grand circular staircase with Manuela. Thoughtfully, she had arranged for us to spend the night in the same room as we had when we were little girls! Now we could talk to our hearts' content. We filled each other in with the latest details of our lives, then quickly turned our thoughts to Pilar. Living in Barcelona, Manuela had kept in touch with our dear friend even though they moved in different circles. I learned that Pilar had become somewhat estranged from her parents as a result of her marriage. At the beginning, it was not easy for her to make ends meet, but gradually she was able to supplement Carlos' income with earnings from her embroidery. In her spare time, she would volunteer to teach fine sewing skills to girls from her neighbourhood.

"You will see many of them at the funeral tomorrow," Manuela predicted.

I finally mustered enough courage to enquire how Pilar had died.

"Childbirth, as so often happens. There was only a midwife to help and I doubt that she was experienced. Pilar must have given birth at least ten times, but most were stillborn."

Manuela paused at the thought of those tragic circumstances. Then she asked me suddenly: "Have you heard about Pilar's eldest son?"

"No. What about him?"

"Well, Pablo is only fourteen but he plays the cello so beautifully that all Barcelona is raving about it. He has even gone to Madrid to play for Queen Isabella."

"Pilar must have been very proud of him."

"Of course both parents were delighted with their son's ability, but Carlos was weary of the musician's hardships and wanted him, at first, to learn another trade. Pilar, on the other hand, was convinced of Pablo's exceptional talent right from the beginning. She made all kinds of sacrifices so he could study with the best teachers. She was totally devoted to him."

"It must have been hard for Pilar not to see him become fully established."

"Oh, absolutely. By an amazing coincidence, I was at her bedside when she passed away." Manuela spoke very slowly as she recalled Pilar's last moments. "She had a high fever but was fully conscious. Carlos and Pablo were holding her hands when she told us her last wish."

"What did she say?" I couldn't help asking.

"You will hear it at the funeral," Manuela answered evasively. I knew I shouldn't press her.

Rain was falling steadily when we arrived for the funeral. The little church with its crumbling walls was close to where Pilar and Carlos lived, according to Manuela. It was sparsely furnished, its windows unadorned with the usual stained glass. There was no organ, just an upright piano which I assumed that Carlos would normally play. But overcome with grief, he was replaced today by Senor Morales, his old professor. I saw that Pilar's parents had come, too, in spite of their differences with her. They were sitting uneasily in the second row just behind Carlos and the children. Many young people were also there, some no doubt Carlos' students and some perhaps the girls who learned sewing from Pilar, as Manuela had mentioned. In front of the altar stood the plain casket with a modest wreath of carnations. My thoughts turned once again to the evening fifteen years ago when Pilar had given away her elegant clothes so dramatically.

A young priest conducted Mass and recited with diligence the familiar liturgy. The small choir sang softly amid flickering candles and a pall of gloom descended on the mourners. As the service was coming to an end, the priest turned to the casket and raised both hands:

"Beloved sister Pilar, I now commend your soul to Jesus, Our Lord. May you rest in peace. May your soul and the souls of all the faithful departed, through the mercy of God, rest in peace. Amen"

After a pause, he faced the congregation and resumed: "It is my understanding that before she passed away, Senora Casals had made a special request. I am pleased to fulfill her last wish now by asking her son Pablo to perform for us."

Manuela looked at me with a knowing smile.

Confidently, a boy stepped forward, looking unusually mature for his age. Dwarfed by the cello he was holding, he bowed gently towards the audience and glanced over to Senor Morales, the accompanist at the piano. Then he sat down and began to play a soulful melody by Dvořák. It was a piece often sung in concerts and I knew the lyrics well:

Songs my mother taught me, in the days long vanish'd,
seldom from her eyelids were the teardrops banish'd.

But now, without words, Pablo was conveying the lingering regret even more forcefully with his sensitive playing. This was clearly a grieving son's heartfelt tribute to his mother. Like many others around me, I was moved to tears. Little did we know that an even greater emotional experience was in store for us.

The next piece started with an easily recognizable accompaniment on the piano and I knew immediately that Pablo was going to play *The Swan*. At first, I assumed that this graceful composition by Saint-Saens was meant to be a portrait of Pilar. But when the cello entered, I shivered with the realization that it was actually Pilar *speaking* to us. So, this was to be her Swan Song! Of all the stringed instruments, the cello is closest to the human voice, especially when played in the cantabile or singing style as Pablo did. He had also chosen an exceptionally slow tempo that transformed the easy-flowing melody into a plaintive chant. In this way, what started out as a gentle melancholy turned relentlessly into heart-rending sorrow. It reached a shattering climax in the form of a sustained high note filled with unbearable anguish. It seemed as if Pilar was lashing out at the cruelty of fate. I thought to myself, how dreadful it must be to depart this life with so much resentment. But suddenly, something of a miracle happened. In the space of two bars, the music became infused with a wonderful sense of consolation. When the cello brought the piece to a close with four drawn-out notes, all was serenity and grace. I was completely puzzled. What had been powerful enough to give her such consolation?

By now, the procession carrying the casket was ready to leave the church. As the grieving family passed by, I caught a glimpse of the quiet determination on Pablo's face and in an instant, found the answer to my question. Even in her deepest despair, Pilar was fully convinced that her son would become a great musician. His success would be the fulfillment of her life and her ultimate consolation! As the church door opened, brilliant sunshine came flooding in.

Author's Note

Pablo Casals (1876-1973) was born in the Catalan province of Spain and became the most prominent cellist of his time in the world. This is a largely fictional account of the life of Pablo Casals' mother, Pilar Defilló de Casals. However, I have tried to stay true to her character as revealed in Pablo Casals' memoirs (*Joys and Sorrows, Reflections by Pablo Casals*, ed. A. E. Kahn, Simon and Schuster, New York 1970). She recognised her son's extraordinary talents early on and cheerfully made sacrifices and endured hardships to support him. In my story, I imagined the tragedy that would have occurred if she had been unable to witness the great success of his career. In the circumstances of those days, women faced the prospect of death from childbirth many times in their lives. I am happy to inform the reader that in reality she lived to a ripe old age and her son was extremely devoted to her.

TRAINS TO LOS ANGELES

Rachel Harvey

As I SIT HERE, MY OLD HANDS CRAMPING around this pen, I'm determined to record my story, the way I remember it now, for my children and their children. Lord knows there are many different accounts of me, my husband, and our lives. This is mine ...

Summer, 1924

My sister Hazel had been sending me letters every few days for a month. She lived in Los Angeles with her husband, Harold, and I think she was feeling lonely. Not that Harold didn't make good company for her, but she was longing for some female companionship, a girl friend to talk with. Hazel and I were always very close.

I grew up, the youngest of the ten Bounds children, on a Nimi'ipuu reserve in Idaho – the Nez Perce Indian Reservation – where my father worked as a blacksmith. Most of my siblings moved away and started their own families; I remained with my parents. I was approaching my twenty-fourth birthday, and although I knew that it would soon be time for me to "grow up", there was a part of me that was hesitant. I had always been very shy and found it hard to take that next step towards independence. Life here was so quiet, I sometimes thought I might be using the inactivity of the place as an excuse to be inactive in creating my "own life".

Lately however, I was feeling slightly restless, ready for a change.

One day I decided to go for a walk, and headed toward the mailbox at the end of the lane. Sure enough, I had received another letter from Hazel.

Dearest Lillian,

Oh how I miss you! The weather is absolutely wonderful here. And the lights at night … you've never seen anything like it! Won't you join me and Harold here? For once, don't think about it, just do it. Finding work won't be a problem – you'll be working within a few weeks. In the meantime, I'll set up a cot for you in our guest bedroom. Say you'll come! We'll talk soon, dear sister.

Lovingly, Hazel

I walked back toward the house, ruminating on the letter. Hazel made Los Angeles sound so exciting, so … tempting. Maybe I should go. I do need to do *something* with my life. What better time than now? As my mind reeled I picked up the pace, and by the time I reached the house my breath came out in short gasps. Mom, concluding that I must have news, asked if I had heard from Hazel. I thrust the letter at her: "Yes!"

Needless to say, my parents were a bit apprehensive at first, but knowing I would be staying with Hazel eased their worry. Mom said she thought it would be good for me to get out and try something new Dad nodded. So, as quickly as the idea came into being it was settled. I was going to Los Angeles!

Mom and Dad drove me to the station, and after tearful goodbyes, I boarded the train and found my seat. The whistle sounded and soon we chugged forward. The train rattled on the tracks, the steady "click-clacking" noise eventually lulling most of its passengers into a restless sleep. I, on the other hand, could not sleep. The anticipation of the unknown was creating such a nervous feeling in my stomach – I was glad that my seat was close to the washroom. There was no going back now, though. And although my nerves were shot, I knew that going to Los Angeles was a new beginning for me. I could feel the excitement of the unknown boiling up inside of me, like a kettle that was seconds away from whistling.

Destination: Los Angeles

The train steamed forward through the state of Nevada's dry, cracking desert land, and soon the cityscape of Los Angeles sprouted on the horizon like some strange and leafless desert plant. When we finally pulled into the station, I peered through the window to see Hazel eagerly waving her arms, front and centre on the platform, and I scooped my belongings and rushed to embrace her.

"Here I am!" I announced, grinning.

We entered the 'outside world', and I was surprised by the mass of vehicles that surrounded me. Exhaust fumes filled my nostrils as I peered up at the mirage of skyscrapers, immediately feeling a touch of vertigo. Hazel instantly grabbed my hand and led me to a taxi. As quickly as I was introduced to the madness of the city I was contained once again as a traveler, with a mere view of the excitement.

The drive was a short one, and within no time the taxi halted in front of a small apartment building in need of a fresh coat of paint. The cot I slept on had a metal bar that poked my back so that I had to sleep on my side, or else wake up with a backache. The apartment was clean and plain, but we always had enough to eat and Hazel's description of the lights at night was very true. The view of the city from the rickety balcony was picturesque, in a postcard sort of way, with buildings, streets, palm trees and people all illuminated in a sort of blurred, unexpected beauty. There was an air of excitement here, something new that I had never felt back home in Idaho.

I was hesitant to go outside the apartment on my own at first, however, one day, very bored with life indoors, I ventured out for a walk around town. I ran into Ruth, one of Hazel's friends I had been introduced to at the apartment the week before. Ruth suggested we eat lunch together, and while we chatted she mentioned there was a job opening at the studio of Walt Disney, where she currently worked inking film frames. The job paid $15 a week, which was more than I had ever earned before, and Ruth invited me to come to the studio the next day and apply. I was thrilled at the prospect.

The Disney Studio

The best part about the idea of working at the studio was that it was within walking distance of the apartment. The studio itself was small; however, I was fascinated by all of the animation cels which covered every inch of the walls. This was certainly the most colorful place I had ever seen! After meeting with a man named Roy (who I later discovered was Walt's brother), I was informed that the job was mine. Hazel, Ruth and I celebrated that night by going to see a movie at the theatre. Things were finally looking up!

At the Disney Studio I was kept busy all day and sometimes into the night. The ink stained my hands, so that when I was finished for the day I had colored fingertips. But I quickly adjusted to the fast-paced setting, because I felt inspired. I also was responsible for secretarial duties at the studio, and was glad that the job provided me with a chance to be creative as well as to put my much-praised organizational skills to use.

Shortly after I started at the studio, I met Mr. Disney. He was quite handsome, and what an imagination he had! He seemed to be very interested in what *I* had to say, as well. I found it surprising and, honestly, quite refreshing the way he hung on every word as I told him stories of my childhood. I wondered if maybe he could be a romantic prospect for me. Time would tell, I supposed.

The Charming Walt Disney

One day after work, Walt – he'd requested that I address him by his first name, as he felt Mr. Disney was too formal – asked me if I would accompany him on a car ride. I agreed. We talked about many things, and he confided in me about his business dealings and goings on. I was flattered that he felt he could talk to me and told him the honest truth when he asked for my opinion. The car rides became a regular occurrence.

Walt hadn't officially called on me up to this point, because he had been struggling financially and did not own a suit. Once Walt and Roy, who was also his business partner, started earning some profits from the Disney enterprise, both men went out and bought new clothes. The evening after he purchased his suit, Walt came calling for me. He 'strutted' into Hazel's apartment, obviously very proud of his new attire. Hazel, Harold, and our cousin Madeline, who was now living with us too, all took an immediate liking to Walt. We all hoped he was "the one" for me. So, when he proposed marriage to me a few weeks later, I did not hesitate to give him my answer: "Yes!"

1925: Mrs. Lillian Disney

We had a small wedding at my uncle's house in Idaho. But we were happy, and as soon as time permitted, we went on a honeymoon cruise together. Walt always had work on his mind though, and the idea of relaxing and 'just doing nothing' did not appeal to him for long. From the moment I met him I knew that his passion for what he did was a top priority. But his passion had grown to be a huge part of my life as well. I quickly became almost as determined as he was to see his vision turn to reality – to see Disney Studios accomplish great success.

1927: Oswald the Rabbit

Once we were settled in a new apartment, Walt began to work constantly, and within no time he had a contract with a Mr. Mintz in New York for a character he created named Oswald the Rabbit. I was so pleased when Walt gave me the news of Oswald's success, and was especially enthusiastic about his wage increase. (We were not well-off at that point and any bit of extra money helped.)

Walt later discovered that Mintz had hidden the fact that *he* owned the rights to Oswald, and not Walt, the creator. This revelation made Walt very unhappy, and we discussed this each night upon his return from work. He debated whether to go to New York at Mintz's request to possibly sign a further contract for Oswald. I suggested it would be a good idea to at least see what the options were, and Walt agreed, inviting me along for the trip.

1928: A Star is Born

Once again, I found myself on a train, this time from Los Angeles to New York. To me there was just something inherently exciting about a train ride. Things always seemed to happen when I arrived at my destination. New and unexpected things. And once again I had a premonition that our lives would change with this trip.

When we arrived in New York, Walt and I checked into a hotel and had lunch with Mr. Mintz and his wife. Mintz introduced Walt as an up-and-coming animator to many high profile people in the media industry. When it came time for Walt to meet with Mr. Mintz to discuss the business of Oswald's future, Walt suggested I go shopping around town and I was glad to oblige, as this was quite a treat for me.

When I met Walt for dinner that night, he looked rather distraught.

"Lillian, my dear," he confided, "it appears I have a tough decision to make."

Walt explained that Mintz had offered him a very low sum of money to keep Walt's name on the character of Oswald the Rabbit, and if he did not accept the deal, Mintz had arranged for many of the workers at the Disney Studio to work for him now, using higher wages as a bargaining tool. This was grave news indeed. After some discussion, Walt decided he would give Oswald completely to Mintz, and find a new character for himself. We decided to leave for home in the morning.

On the train ride home, Walt was smoking one cigarette after another, and I ordered a glass of wine to help ease the butterflies in my stomach. There was something in the way Walt was acting; I could see the wheels turning in his head. He was so disappointed, but he never let that show. Instead, he began sketching in his notebook almost as soon as the train departed, drawing aimless lines and shapes on the notepaper. Eventually, the shapes started to take form, and before long I could see that he'd drawn a cartoon mouse. He later told me that the mouse idea came to him when he recalled living in an old, run-down apartment in Kansas before he had even come to Los Angeles. He'd had many "mouse friends" there, and suddenly it struck him that a mouse should be his next character. I rather liked the idea myself, but when he told me that the character's name would be Mortimer Mouse, I had my doubts. I sat for a moment, contemplating, and soon responded "Mortimer seems too formal, too sissy. How about Mickey? Mickey Mouse?"

Walt liked the name, and that settled it. Mickey Mouse it was. Excitement bubbled over in both of us the rest of the train ride home. Upon arrival, Walt and I hurried to gather our things like school children dismissed after a long day of school and went straight back to the studio. Scrounging up what food I could find, I prepared a meal for us right there while Walt called Roy and discussed the idea for this new character. Walt was no longer distraught over losing Oswald; he was too exuberant over the new idea of Mickey and went full steam ahead with his plans. And so an important part of Disney history was made.

1997: Looking Back

I always treasured the way Walt never let setbacks slow him down. He was a survivor, a determined businessman, and forever young at heart. Two years his senior, I used to tease him that I had more experience in the ways of life and therefore could give him valuable advice on his ideas. Walt, in fact, took this seriously as I became his "sounding board" of sorts. But I wasn't always right. When he came up with the idea to build an entire theme park, I was doubtful at first. It took me awhile to see it, but eventually I did.

I can see that every hardship and every joyous event in my life was part of a journey, this journey to which I find myself nearing the end. At 97 years of age, I wonder if I will live to see 100. I won't be sad if in fact I don't reach the century mark, because my life has been so full. I had the privilege of raising two wonderful daughters, and in turn the pleasures of seeing their children grow, and I have been fortunate enough to find love a second time after Walt passed. I got to see Walt Disney World become a reality and am sure Walt would have approved.

I would like to see the Concert Hall fully built, though, before I pass on. Walt would be proud to see his name attached to as worthy a project as the Los Angeles Philharmonic. "Music makes my films take flight," he used to say.

His name has been attached to many great projects, and I am proud to have been part of them. But the moments I remember most vividly are those life-changing train rides to Los Angeles.

Author's Note

When I first set out to write about Walt Disney's wife, I had no idea what to expect. Would there be enough information available about Lillian? Was there a story there? But I quickly found that there were plenty of resources, both online and at my local library, which referred specifically to Lillian.

I became intrigued when I discovered that it was in fact Lillian who had come up with the name for Mickey Mouse. Although she was definitely a 'behind the scenes' kind of person, often choosing to avoid media attention, she evidently played an instrumental role, not only in Walt's personal life but also in his business, lending valuable criticisms to his countless ideas. She was his advisor, friend, lover, and supporter to the end, outliving him by 31 years … what a woman!

Lillian Bounds Disney, 1899-1997

REFLECTIONS IN A CUP OF TEA

Jane Devries

An aromatic blend of fresh bread and spiced meats floats in through the open balcony door. I know that smell to mean that it's ten a.m. The trolleys roll along the street, taking goods to the Gaza Market. The door to our kitchen opens. Anjeylla enters the den and quietly places a tray on the desk beside me.

"Will there be one cup or two this morning, mum?"

I smile and tell her that one will do. She nods and bows low, as she gathers the extra china from the tray. She slips out of the room as silently as she'd arrived. Her question plays over in my head. I'm sure I hear some of my 'Canadian' in her accent. Anjeylla has been with Ted and me for over ten years, since my reluctant retirement. I'm still not comfortable with having help, but a long career in nursing gave me the instinct to recognize when it was no longer prudent to try and manage alone.

Ted is still going strong, canvassing for vaccines and improved medical programs. He has passed along much of the work to younger doctors, but he is keen on keeping up the pressure, as long as his health allows. Ted's latest saying is, "We can't leave everything to the young doctors. They don't have the time that we older, retired guys have." I smile to myself when I hear him go on, as I recall the days when he'd say that fighting for medical programs can't be left to the old guys because they just don't have the energy.

Later this evening, Ted will be back from presenting a keynote speech in Paris. He's been gone for two days. After forty-two years of marriage, I still long for him when he's away.

In many ways Ted reminds me of my father. I can still picture Father, rallying support for the Canadian Medical system. Medicare. Fair treatment of workers. Job security. So many causes, so many speeches. All through my childhood, my father was considered to be a rebellious outsider. Many times, during my teen-aged years particularly, I'd spend half the night wishing that he'd just relax and try to coast a bit. But, blending in and coasting weren't things that Tommy Douglas had on his mind; my prayers went unanswered.

As similar as they are in their zeal and idealism, however, they are also very different men. With my husband, I only ever felt pride and love. His convictions drew me to him in the first place, and I grow to love him more each day. Even now a warmth rushes over me as I think of him.

My father evoked a wide variety of emotions. Early on, when the Douglases first adopted me, I was bewildered and awed by my new family. I was a playmate – a toy, really – for my older sister, Shirley. But my father and mother made sure, out of sheer strength of will, that I never felt myself to be anything less than family. "And who is this?" one of the multitude of politicians or union heads would ask. "My daughter," my father would reply with a sternness that indicated that the subject was closed. First, there was one daughter, now there were two. I was his daughter, and no one was permitted to suggest differently.

I stand up to stretch my legs, and breathe in the scent of the herbal tea. All of these reminiscences of my childhood make me appreciate my current surroundings. At this time of year, the cold dampness of Ottawa or the frigid conditions of Saskatchewan just don't compare with the dry, warm air of Israel. Still, there is something to say for making the year's first snowman and believing in a Santa Claus who rides a sleigh along snow-covered roofs. The children here wouldn't be able to understand how different winter was when I was a little girl.

Many of these children have gone through a lot. When we arrived many, many years ago, Ted and I found work in the Hadassah Hospital as a means of financing our world-wide travel plans. We've been stationed in Israel ever since.

I pour some tea through the filter, then tap it lightly on the edge of the cup, trying to coax all of the water through the fragrant leaves. The china, classic blue Royal Doulton, clinks delicately as I lift my cup from the plate. I let the steam billow in my face as I sip. The set was a gift from Shirley, and her son, Keifer. Twelve place settings of bone china out here on the strip. Those two must have so much money, they've forgotten how to be reasonable. At first I thought Shirley'd lost her mind and forgotten who I was. What would a girl from Saskatchewan want with this breakable, dainty china? It cost them a fortune to get it here. I was throwing out packaging for days.

As is always the case, Shirley knew me better than I knew myself. I fell in love with the set and absorbed it into my daily routine. On days when that routine involved putting people back together in an understaffed emergency room, the set offered a contrast of quiet dignity and composure.

And, every day at tea, I think of them over in California – or wherever their work has taken them last. I hear of them from the kids. I guess Keifer's landed a big part in a television series, "Twenty Four Hours" or some such thing. The kids read about him on the internet. It will never cease to astound me how small the world has become.

My mind goes back to the early days. When I concentrate, I can almost feel again what it was like to be in a young body, free of cares and pain.

Back then, you were either a fan of Tommy Douglas, or you weren't. There was no grey area with my father. Shirley and I could gauge the political tide by standing on the playground. It made us tough. We stuck together as stubbornly as our parents would have expected. Father's ideas were good ones. They were well intended, and we stood behind him. It wasn't always easy.

I sought anonymity, at least so I thought. Though if I'd hated the crowds as much as I told my mother, I probably wouldn't have married Ted and spent my life with him, rallying support for better health-care in Israel. Israel, not Canada, which was home to my parents. Not Hollywood or Broadway, which has become home to Shirley. Our home is here.

I don't know how Shirley can endure all the traveling she has to do. I long ago lost the bug. Following Father on his tours, we've dragged suitcases across almost every main street in the Canadian prairies. As the Douglas name gained notoriety, the trips became longer, but less frequent – at least less frequent for us girls. Most of the trips, Father took without us as Mother made it her mission to give us as normal a life as possible.

I hold the tea close and allow the scent of it to drift past my face.

I wonder why I chose nursing and how I found myself so at home in a country riddled with war and unrest. Was it Father's influence, the example of his constant battle for Medicare? No, I expect that it was Shirley, with her yen for drama and crowds who was influenced by him. Nursing is a quietly thankless career involving care, organization and management – all traits for which Irma Douglas should be famous. Father was named Canadian of the Year, but it was Mother who made that possible. Father always gave her credit. He had to credit her, her contribution was obvious to all who knew us well. She was the one who kept us together, she was the glue. She monitored Father's health and, when he had worn himself too thin, she stepped in and forced his recovery. If she felt that he needed rest, no one – no matter their political power – was permitted to interrupt his time at home. She watched over Shirley and me with the same vigilance.

The floor lifts in a wave under my feet, and I barely have time to begin my fall to my knees when the flat explodes in a blood-curdling bang. The noise is so intense, I can only feel my scream rip through my throat; the sound of it never penetrates my ears. A deafening silence follows. The world holds its breath. A dream? No. Sirens ring in the distance. Closer by, Anjeylla begins to shriek and shriek.

No, not in my neighbourhood. "This won't do!" I holler over her screams.

Anjeylla's cries subside somewhat; she probably figures I've gone insane. That's fine with me, if it keeps her from panicking.

"Anjeylla, get my bag," I demand. I use my arms to haul my old bones up off the floor. As I lift my foot, I hear it come down on the dusty, broken handle of my china cup. "And SOMEBODY owes me another china cup," I yell. I am furious. I pull on my sweater, slip out of my slippers – careful not to step on any broken glass – and meet Anjeylla at the door.

"Are you sure?" she asks, obviously knowing the answer, since she is holding the keys and busily pulling on her shoes.

I pull on my walking shoes, and bend to open the medical bag at Anjeylla's feet. I have enough for five – maybe eight – medium wounds. Knowing the time of day, and guessing the location, I know it won't be enough. I reach into the closet and pull out a silk scarf – another gift, this time from the kids. It'll make a decent tourniquet. The tourniquets I've already got can be ripped into more bandages. I curse myself for not keeping a better stock.

We weave through the people standing or running in the apartment's halls. Those who stand, I try to get sitting or assign them to knock on doors and check on the neighbours. The diversion may work to help them stay calm. There's no benefit to rushing to the scene if I simply go past people in my own building who are in shock. We scurry out the doors and through the clouds of dust. Any hope that the explosion didn't take place at the Market fades as the path of smoke and dust leads us right to the square.

I hand Anjeylla a cloth and motion for her to cover her face. She doesn't need the advice; the cloth is readily accepted.

A blackened, flame-ridden car is at the center of the chaos. No use looking inside it. My eye scans the scene, and I've instantly got things prioritized and organized. There's no one here yet – no one in charge, that is – so I grab Anjeylla and haul her over to the closest victim. Among other things, he's a possible – no probable – neck injury.

"Make him stay put. Tell him the ambulance is on the way, and that you'll ensure he's taken care of." This will ease my mind more than his, but I can't have her falling to pieces. For him, I can only hope that seeing her beautiful face will keep him here. On to the others.

With a stream of commands to witnesses and a flurry of white bandages, I work my way down the triage list. After what seems a lifetime, the paramedics descend on the scene. I hand over the patients, and point out those I elected to skip over. The one med nods solemnly at the dead, then hastens into action. I make my way back to the edge of the crowd and help Anjeylla gather what's left of my kit.

She holds my arm, as we hobble home. Everything hurts. No exclusions. With each step, my knees creak, and I groan in pain. Ted will be full of warnings about my health, but he will beam with pride. I have to hurry home, in case he calls.

I've lost my scarf. I can't re … oh, yes. I remember now. It served as a good tourniquet, just as I'd expected. I must send the kids my thanks.

At the door, Anjeylla hesitates and eyes me carefully as she slowly lets go of my arm. She fumbles with the key.

"Shall we try for tea, again?" I ask. "I believe we both deserve one." She nods.

Home is where you are needed. This, I know, is my home.

Author's Note

I wrote "Reflections in a Cup of Tea" in response to a class assignment: "Write a fictional story about a real woman – one who is related to a famous man." Having been recently inundated with stories of Tommy Douglas after his being voted "The Greatest Canadian" in a nationally televised contest organized by the CBC, I found the assignment to be a great opportunity to write about his youngest daughter, Joan. Searches on the internet (NDP archives, wikipedia.org, CBC.ca and other sites) found scant references to this member of Tommy's family. On wikipedia, her reference is "… and they later adopted a second daughter Joan, who became a nurse". "Reflections in a Cup of Tea" is a story which creates a rich, happy life for Tommy Douglas' second daughter. It is what the author hopes she has achieved.

THE RANI OF JHANSI, 'BRAVEST OF THE REBELS'

Waheed Rabbani

IT IS SAID THAT NATIONS SHOULD never forget those who give up their lives fighting for the freedom of their country. Unfortunately, the history texts used in the schools formerly administered by the British in India only mention in passing the heroism of those who rose in 1857, to initiate that nation's struggle for freedom. India's remembrance of her martyrs needs attention.

One of these martyrs is Rani Lakshmibai of the former kingdom of Jhansi, whose glorious courage won grudging admiration even from her enemy. The Rani's death was mentioned in the report of the final battle dispatched by the Commander of the British Force, Sir General Hugh Rose, to the Governor General, as follows:

> *I have the honour ... to draw His Excellency's attention particularly to the great gallantry and devotion displayed by Her Majesty's 8th Hussars, in the brilliant charge which they made through the enemy's Camp; of which one most important result was the death of the Ranee of Jhansi; who, although a lady, was the bravest and best Military leader of the Rebels.*

On November 19th, 1828, in Varanasi, a girl was born to a Brahmin family. Mannikarnika or Manu, was the name given to her. Unfortunately, her mother died when Manu was only four; hence, the responsibility of the young girl's upbringing fell on the father. Her father, although not of high means – he was in the employ of the brother of the Raja of the state neighbouring Jhansi – took up the task with enthusiasm. Through his efforts, her education comprised not only bookwork, but also horseback riding, sword fighting, and even musket firing.

India was then governed – in the collection of taxes, keeping of an Army and other administrative matters – by the British East India Company, through the Governor General who also looked after legal affairs. At that time, James Andrew Broun-Ramsay, also known as the 1st Marquess of Dalhousie, held that position. In those days India was made up of many kingdoms and principalities and each dealt with the British East India Company (British) individually. Jhansi was one of those ruled, not by the British, but by their own monarch, the Raja. The Maharaja of Jhansi had maintained a pro-British policy throughout his reign. After the 1817 defeat by the British of the Maratha Confederacy, a treaty granted the kingdom of Jhansi to the Raja's heirs and successors in perpetuity. The British even conferred upon him the title of 'Maharaja' for his support in the Burma Wars.

With the passage of time, and with an eye to expansion, the British Government instituted a policy of 'Lapse,' whereby when an Indian ruler died without an heir, the principality would be annexed under direct British administration. Lord Dalhousie extended the policy to include rulers with adopted children as well, declaring that adoptees could not be legal heirs. This decree was in direct conflict with the Indian belief that an adopted child is the equal of a child by birth. This denial of the legitimacy of an adopted son offended Indian sentiments.

In 1842, when Mannikarnika was at the tender age of fourteen, her father received a proposal for marriage from Gangadhar Rao, the Maharaja of Jhansi. The Maharaja was at an advanced age and still childless from earlier marriages. No doubt being aware of the policy of Lapse, he was anxious for an heir. An astrologer, called to review the marriage prospects, deemed the match excellent and announced that the girl possessed the combined qualities of three Hindu goddesses: Lakshmi, the goddess of wealth and beauty; Durga, the goddess of bravery and Saraswati, the goddess of intelligence. After her marriage, she was given the name Lakshmibai. The renaming might also have meant to reflect the fact that she was very beautiful, much like the image of the goddess Lakshmi.

Laksmibai did not let the title of Rani go to her head. Instead of leading a life of luxury and idleness in the opulent surroundings of the palace, she took a keen interest in the affairs of the kingdom and devoted her time to art and literature. As she was fond of riding, she devised an ingenious way to fulfill that desire. After much imploring of the Maharaja, she received his reluctant permission to raise a small cavalry regiment composed only of women. She garbed them in colorful uniforms and drilled them every morning at daybreak. The town residents flocked to the parade grounds to see, likely in amusement, this unusual sight of a group of females performing maneuvers on horseback and learning to charge, thrust and parry with their talwars. This was the first cavalry regiment of its kind in India.

It would seem that the gods were kind to her – for a while anyway. To the great joy of the Maharaja and indeed the whole kingdom of Jhansi, Rani Lakshmibai gave birth to a son in 1851. However, the celebrations had hardly abated, when misfortune fell; the child died just four months after his birth. As a result of this tragedy, the Maharaja fell into depression and his already poor health worsened so much that he grew critically ill. Mindful of the future of his kingdom, in the presence of the British Resident and the Captain of a small British force stationed outside the city, he adopted a five-year-old boy, a cousin named Damodar Rao. As if fulfilling a premonition, the Maharaja died in November 1853, just a few days after the adoption of Damodar. Upon the death of the Maharaja, Rani Lakshmibai, at the young age of twenty-five, was left to run her kingdom as titular head until her adopted son came of age. The Rani did not lose heart, and dealt with her duties and responsibilities admirably. She also continued to devote time to her women's cavalry regiment. There was peace and prosperity in her lands.

News of the Maharaja's death eventually reached Lord Dalhousie. Although, as per Hindu tradition, little Damodar Rao had been willed by the Maharaja as his heir and successor, the British ruler rejected the Rani's claim that Damodar Rao was the legal heir. She made several petitions, arguing that the heir was a relative of the Maharaja, and that British officers had witnessed the adoption ceremony. She pointed to the treaty with the British Government and further argued that the Lapse doctrine should not apply to Jhansi, as it was an ancient hereditary kingdom of India. A visiting Australian Lawyer, Arthur Lang, whom the Rani had hired at great expense, presented her appeals to the Governor General in Calcutta and even took her case all the way to London. All the petitions fell on deaf ears. Lord Dalhousie applied Lapse and annexed Jhansi into British territory. The populace was horrified on learning this news. They were particularly distressed that the British were using Jhansi's misfortune to expand their Empire.

However, in March 1854 in consideration of the annexation, Lord Dalhousie announced an annual pension of 60,000 Rupees (about $1,000) for the Rani. An envoy arrived from Calcutta with this offer and orders for her to leave the Jhansi fort and take up residence in a smaller house in town. The Rani received the British delegation ceremonially, in a *darbar* (full court), and read the offer of the "gracious" pension and the eviction notice. The pension was tempting, as it offered her and her son a scanty subsistence. Some might have considered it generous, and other heads of states had accepted such offers. However, the Rani was determined not to turn her back on Jhansi. She believed it was her duty to stand up not only for her rights, but those of her son and her kingdom, and indeed for all the natives of India. To the astonishment of Lord Dalhousie's representatives, the Rani tore up the letter and threw it on the court's white marble floor, while the elder members of her assembly looked at her with pride. When the head of the British delegation asked for her reply to the Governor General, she stood up from her throne, raised the curved sword she always carried, and declared, "*I shall never give up my Jhansi.*" She then ordered her palace guards and the women's cavalry to escort the British envoys out of the fort.

Fearing violence, the British enlarged their military presence at Jhansi. A cantonment town was set up on the plains outside the Jhansi fort walls. The British advised the Rani to move out of the fort to the house in town, from whence she could run the town administratively, placing Jhansi outside the jurisdiction of the British courts. Lakshmibai agreed to this compromised arrangement and the British occupied the fort. She, however, continued to write letters to various British officials pleading the case for her adopted son. She felt that by keeping the channels of communication open, she might still make Damodar the Maharaja of Jhansi.

Three years passed and in May of 1857 the Rani came close to achieving her desire. The sepoys (Indian soldiers in the service of the British) mutinied. It started in the northern town of Merut and spread like wildfire across central India in the military cantonments along the Ganges River. In several cases barracks were burned and British officers and their families slaughtered. In some places, such as at Kanpur, the British were permitted free passage to the British capital of Calcutta. However, sepoys along the banks of the river started shooting at the boats carrying the Europeans. Most of the wooden boats caught fire and their occupants perished. Only one of the numerous boats managed to sail away, hotly pursued by rebels. Just four officers of the large Kanpur contingent of nearly one thousand men, women and children managed to reach safety.

The Great Indian Sepoy Rebellion engulfed the small British garrison at the Jhansi fort as well. However there, after the sepoys mutinied, most the British officers and their families managed to flee inside the fort and bar the gates. They remained holed-up inside the fort for nearly a week. There was heavy exchange of cannon and musket fire as the rebels tried to storm the walls. Finally, with food and water running low, the British soldiers surrendered to the rebels, possibly having been offered safe passage to another town. However, after they were led out of the fort, the sepoys attacked and killed all sixty-six men, women and children. The Sepoy rebels then left Jhansi and marched towards Delhi, which their comrades had captured. They had proclaimed Bhadhur Shah Zafar as the new Emperor of India. Historians call him 'The Last Mughal', for his reign lasted only a few months.

The Rani was horrified to learn of these events. She was not an instigator of the mutiny – the sepoys themselves played that role. Although the British historical accounts paint her as siding with the rebels, which she eventually did, there is widespread folkloric belief that she was a caring, loving person and on no account would have ordered the killing of the sixty-six British men, women and children. In fact some eyewitness accounts by native servants of the British families tell of her sending food and water to the besieged Europeans. However, the British military labeled her a rebel and held her responsible for the murders. Hence, given the British counter attacks on the rebel stronghold cities such as Delhi, Kanpur and Lucknow, along with severe reprisals and mass hangings of rebels and innocent civilians alike, the Rani knew that it was only a matter of time until her Jhansi would be attacked.

In anticipation of this, Rani Lakshmibai strengthened the defenses of her fort and assembled a volunteer army. A large number of women joined up and were given military training along with the men. She thus collected a force of brave warriors from the local population of Jhansi, irrespective of their religion or caste. They were willing to fight to the end and give up their lives for the cause of Independence and for their beloved Rani.

In March 1858, a large British force lead by General Sir Hugh Rose arrived and laid siege to Jhansi. General Rose first offered a chance to surrender; however, the Rani, when all her faithful warriors voted to fight, turned it down, and the inevitable heavy shelling commenced. The rebels stood firm and returned fire from the ramparts. The fighting incurred heavy casualties on both sides. Inside the fort, despite the dire situation, the spirits of the population remained high. The Jhansi women and children helped by carrying ammunition and food to the soldiers. Rani Lakshmibai herself was on the ramparts daily, inspecting the defenses of the city and weighing the advice of her commanders. The fort's walls – six to eight feet thick and twenty feet high – held up to the bombardment and the rebels were able to repulse many attacks from the British.

After more than a week of mounting casualties, the British soldiers seemed to be getting demoralized. General Rose was furious at their failure to breach the fort walls. He also feared that his troops would not be able to withstand a counterattack should the Rani mount one.

Jhansi did receive some help from a rebel leader, Tatia Tope. He arrived with a large force composed mostly of native irregulars; however, the gods were not on his side. General Rose, using only half his forces, drove him across the river in a brilliant nighttime tactical maneuver. The other half continued their siege of the Jhansi fort. Tatia, having lost a large portion of his army, including cannons and supplies, was unable to counterattack. Historians fault the Rani for her one strategic mistake of not having launched a cavalry charge at the British lines in support of Tatia. Despite her still possessing a sizeable cavalry force within the fort walls, she chose not to sally out. She may have misjudged the size of the British force, which after more than two weeks of fighting had been considerably depleted. Others surmise she did not attack because of her very nature. It is well known that she believed in the goodness of the souls of her adversaries. She may have believed the British would give up and go away, making it unnecessary for her to spill more of their blood. And they might have, had it not been for one treacherous person.

In the middle of one moonless night, help came to General Rose in the form of a traitor, a devotee of the half brother of the deceased Maharaja of Jhansi, who believed that the throne should have been his. He made a deal with the General to open one of the lesser-guarded gates of the city walls for the British. In return, it is said that the British bequeathed the traitor two Jhansi villages.

And so it was that on a dark night the British army swarmed into Jhansi. Again Rani Lakshmibai, did not lose heart. Dressed as a man and full of courage and patriotism, she fought the enemy alongside her warriors. Some say that she had her son, Damodar Rao, strapped tightly behind her. Others record that she held the reins of her horse in her mouth and fenced valiantly, a sword in each hand.

The element of surprise was on the side of the invaders. Many Jhansi soldiers were cut down sleeping in their cots. The situation became desperate as the British soldiers gradually gained control, rampaging through the city and driving the warriors back. It was evident that the city would soon fall. The Rani and her remaining rebels were cornered at one end of the fort. At the behest of her advisors, the Rani ordered her soldiers to lay down their arms and escape if they could. She herself, along with some of her cavalry, left the city. Perhaps it is a myth that she and her group jumped their horses over the fort walls. Part of the wall still stands and a small monument to their bravery marks the exact spot from where they are said to have leapt. Other historians have them sliding down the wall with ropes or simply riding out through a gate.

In any case Rani Lakshmibai and her followers reached the neighboring city of Kalpi where they took refuge. Many other rebellious forces heard of her daring and joined her. Her example inspired a widespread rebellion across the nation. General Rose soon learned of the Rani's whereabouts and directed his force in pursuit. From Kalpi the Rani and the rebels departed for Gwalior, a city atop a mountain, said to be almost impregnable. However, the Raja of Gwalior feared losing his kingdom to the British. An old pensioner, he refused to support the Rani. However, his forces joined the Rani's.

A British contingent was sighted marching towards that fort. In a desperate move, perhaps the strategic action she wished she had employed during the battle at Jhansi, the Rani, with her women's cavalry force and some Pathan warriors (northern tribesmen), decided to charge the British. A fierce battle took place in the plains known as Kotah-ki-Serai. The Rani fought most valiantly in her usual manner, with talwars in both her hands and the reins of the horse in her mouth. It was on the second day of fighting that the great heroine of the first struggle for Indian freedom lost her life. She was surrounded by a group of battle-hardy Hussars – just arrived after service in the Crimea – with whom she parried fiercely. The Hussar who finally killed her with a thrust of his sword into her back, swore that he did not realize they were fighting a woman, for she was not only dressed like a man, but also fought like one. It is said that the entire Hussars' camp was upset at having fought and killed a woman.

It was the 18th of June, 1858. But this was not the end of Rani Lakshmibai's dream of freeing her Jhansi – and India – from British rule; it was the beginning. Her wholehearted determination for the cause she believed in inspired others to take up the struggle. It took another ninety years of resolute effort, and Gandhiji's 'Non-violence Movement' along with the 'Quit India Campaign', for India to gain her Independence in August, 1947. Though Independence Day is celebrated in India with great gusto at midnight every August 14th, the memory of Rani Lakshmibai is fading. Her example of courage and determination appears to be being erased, as if by the wind that gusts along the walls of the Jhansi fort and embraces the statue which stands at the spot where she jumped down the ramparts. There she sits on a rearing horse, her right arm raising a sword. Inscribed at the base of the statue are her words:

I shall never give up my Jhansi

Author's Note

Having been born in India, I had heard about the Rani of Jhansi and her legendary efforts during the start of the Independence movement, but not in any great detail until I started researching for my novel based on the Great Indian Rebellion/Mutiny of 1857. I have traveled extensively throughout India and have peeked down the ramparts of the Jhansi Fort from where the Rani and her entourage made the fabled equestrian jump to escape the invading British force.

AN "UNREMARKABLE" LIFE

Ethel Edey

A HUNDRED YEARS AGO THE LIFE OF any farm woman followed a predictable pattern – work, work and more work. Such a life would have been considered unremarkable. However, upon looking closely at such a life, one can only marvel.

Wearing a dark blue ankle length dress, straight black hair held in place by a matching ribbon, Bertha hurried to the farm yard, the powder dry dirt dusting her black leather boots. Before heading off to school, she must feed the geese and chickens. Each of the nine children had daily chores, and Bertha, being the third youngest, was no exception. Her parents had emigrated from Russia and purchased a small farm in South Dakota. German was spoken at home, but the children were all learning to speak and read English at school. Although she liked school, Bertha went to work after completing Grade 8, to help support an older brother who was studying to be a minister.

At the age of twenty-one, she married Chris, a young man from a nearby community. Chris was adventuresome and Bertha was happy to follow. Soon they moved to Wisconsin to work on a dairy farm. Bertha milked the cows and tended the house for the bachelor dairy farmer. Two years later, she was the mother of a daughter, Adaline, and a son, Wilfred.

Then Chris heard of "free land" in the Peace River country of Northern Alberta in Canada. Chris and Bertha set off, by train, with their two young children, and Bertha's brother and his wife. The seven travel days were spent amusing the children, preparing food for everyone, and watching the passing scenery. The open prairies, reminding her of South Dakota, were comforting. After transferring to the last train in

Edmonton the scenery changed dramatically. Nothing to see but trees, muskeg, and more trees. Where was the farm land?

The Spirit River area was virgin territory and homesteaders were arriving from many countries. The land was covered in trees and there were no amenities like electricity, running water, or telephones. As soon as they arrived, Chris and Bertha's brother each claimed a homestead. It was a dream come true – land of their own.

Now the hard work began. With their savings, Chris and Bertha purchased a cow and the materials to build a log cabin. Until their new home was ready, they lived with her brother's family in a three room log house. Bertha had the qualities needed to make a success of this venture: she was industrious, self sufficient, practical, and had a strong religious faith. Before long, she had several chickens which she coaxed into laying eggs. Now she was able to sell eggs, roasting chickens, and fresh cream to the townsfolk. Bertha kept meticulous records of her sales while Chris made the deliveries and purchased the weekly groceries with the proceeds. The family's vegetables came from Bertha's large productive garden. Her babies nearby, Bertha spent many hours weeding, harvesting, and preserving. She also planted rows of flowers so she could keep a vase of fresh flowers in the house.

The couple picked wild berries in the woods and ravines on their homestead, always keeping a wary eye out for bears. Bertha was very protective of her chickens. One day she spied a coyote stalking the chicken pen looking for an easy meal. Without hesitation, she pulled Chris' hunting rifle off the wall and, with one shot, killed the coyote. After that, her family teasingly called her "Annie Oakley".

Bertha's hobby was her box Brownie camera with which she pictorially recorded their homesteading life. Some of the things she saw fit to photograph were: the sheaf of grain that stood higher than Chris, who was six feet tall; the wheelbarrow full of super-sized cabbages; Chris driving his team of horses; the threshing crew; herself and her dead coyote; the ladies of the Women's Institute; and, of course, the family. One Christmas day, the family grew again, when Bertha gave birth to her last child, Lloyd, who was ten years younger than his brother.

Church was very important to Bertha. In the early homesteading days, the families from the neighbouring farms would gather in Bertha's log cabin for Sunday service. The chairs would be set up in rows and the minister would play his clarinet to guide the hymn-singing. Some socializing, featuring Bertha's delectable berry pies, always followed the service.

Bertha passed on her German roots by speaking German to the children at home and by cooking traditional foods such as kaistrudel and kuchen. When all the chores had been done, she loved to sit beside the coal oil lamp and read. Despite the relative isolation, she always found reading material: the weekly farm newspaper that came by mail from Winnipeg, her Bible, books she borrowed from neighbours or ones the children brought home from school. Education for the children was a high priority. The children either walked or rode the horse three miles to the country schoolhouse. When the time came, arrangements were made for the two oldest children to stay in town so they could attend high school.

As more settlers moved into the area, the town of Spirit River grew, and roads were built. Eventually, party line phones became available, making it much easier to contact friends and neighbours. If Bertha thought too many "busy-bodies" were listening in on the party line when she was talking to her daughter, she would switch to German. She got a chuckle out of hearing the nosy neighbours, hanging up as they could no longer understand what was being said.

Inevitably, the years brought changes. Bertha's eldest son traveled four hundred miles to Edmonton to study carpentry, and her daughter married a local man, who took his own homestead, a short distance away. Chris and Bertha determined they could finally afford to build a larger frame house. Chris, with the help of neighbours, built the new two story house. The new house had picture windows that looked out over the farmyard and even had a second story balcony! Next came electricity. Bertha could now replace her trusty wood stove with an electric one, and the ice box with a refrigerator. Life became significantly easier.

In addition to raising her youngest son, Bertha now had the joy of entertaining her daughter's three children. The grandchildren napped under Bertha's hand-made butterfly quilt. When they stayed over she always made their favourite dinner – pancakes. When everyone was full, Bertha would make one last big pancake, the size of the frying pan, for the dog who loved pancakes as much as the grandchildren did.

Being an accomplished seamstress, Grandma Bertha was called upon to teach her granddaughters how to sew. They spent many hours together sewing new outfits for school or church. Meanwhile, Bertha continued to sell cream, eggs, and chickens to the townsfolk, tend the large garden which she now shared with her daughter, share the milking chores with Chris, and cook for the threshing crew each harvest.

Bertha was always the first to welcome newcomers to the community. When school teachers came from India and Australia, or new managers came to run the local Co-op Store, Bertha would invite them for dinner. When these folks moved on, they continued to correspond with Bertha, and later with her daughter. They never forgot Bertha's welcoming gifts of hospitality and genuine friendship.

When the work of the farm became too much for Chris and Bertha, they decided it was time to move to town. Bertha embraced this change, in the same positive way she had approached the other significant changes in her life. They purchased a lot in town, sold the farm, and moved the house to the town lot. Bertha immediately went to work, planting a new garden with vegetables, flowers, and berries. Freed from farm work, she focused on sewing garments for children in third world countries. Bertha was featured in the local paper one year, when she sewed over one thousand garments for this United Nations program.

Eventually, it was time for yet another move. Chris and Bertha sold their beloved house and moved to the Retirement Lodge. There, with characteristic grace, Bertha saw the positives. She embraced not having to cook and clean and delighted in having family members join her for lunch at the Lodge. After lunch the visitors would be invited to look through the old photographs Bertha kept in a box on the coffee table in her room, each of which would spawn a story.

When Chris and Bertha celebrated their sixtieth wedding anniversary, I traveled a great distance to be there. For the occasion, Bertha made her dress from a piece of silk fabric I had brought her back from Thailand. To mark this milestone, the family had a star named after Chris and Bertha. I like to think this star, and Bertha, watch over me as I try to be as resourceful, positive, and thoughtful of others as my grandmother was throughout her life – a remarkable life indeed.

Author's Note

This is my first foray into the field of creative writing. My goal is to write the untold stories of remarkable Canadian women who, unnoticed and unrecognized, provided the foundation upon which our country was built.

CONTRIBUTORS

Jean Rae Baxter started writing fulltime a dozen years ago, following a career in education. She writes for both adults and young adults. Short story collections *A Twist of Malice* and *Scattered Light*, as well as her literary murder mystery *Looking For Cardenio*, comprise the former category. Increasingly she is turning to young adult historical fiction to tell the story of Canada's past. *Freedom Bound*, released in February 2012, follows *The Way Lies North* and *Broken Trail*, completing her trilogy set during the American Revolution.

Although **William Chan** spent his academic career at McMaster University as a scientist, he kept a long-standing interest in literature and music. After retirement, he took a course in creative writing. The guidance and encouragement he received in that course have induced in him a love of fiction writing. His wife and two grown children have provided a reliable source of readership and a steady stream of helpful criticism.

Jane Devries is a mom, a software tester, and a perpetual student. She writes for relaxation, but some of her work has been published by Naked Ambition Press. She has written a pre-teen mystery and is currently editing the work to fine-tune the technical references. Also in the works is a novel about a woman who is in the process of clearing clutter from her life.

"An Unremarkable Life?" is **Ethel Edey's** first published work. She recently retired from a rewarding career in healthcare administration and hopes retirement will offer more time for writing. She began writing through the Writing Certificate program at McMaster. Her goal is to write the untold stories of remarkable Canadian women who, unnoticed and unrecognized, provided the foundation upon which our country was built.

Joe Girard is an award-winning actor and filmmaker living in Ottawa. His writing has been published in three countries, and a number of poems have received commendation from deviantart.com. He writes music for the bands Ben Caplan and the Casual Smokers, and Hobo Sapiens of which he is a part. His zen gardens were featured in the Hamilton, Ontario art exhibit, Absorb. Follow his growing collection of art at sandzen.deviantart.com/.

Rachel Harvey is a mother of one and loves being a student. After working in administration for several years, she returned to school and recently completed an Honours Bachelor of Arts in English from McMaster University. She has published articles and poetry in *H Magazine*, *The Silhouette*, *Greater Hamilton Musician*, and is a regular editorial contributor for tvguide.ca. On the sly, she writes country songs and enjoys jamming with her band Rachel Strong and the Sentimental Hearts.

Linda Helson is a prize-winning poet and short story writer living in Dundas, Ontario. Her writing has been published in *Main Street, The Hamilton Spectator, Street Names of Hamilton, Ten Stories High, Hard-boiled Love, Nine Modern Muses* and *Country Connection Magazine.* As well, she edited *Beyond Paradise: An Architectural History of Dundas*, and contributed to *William Lyon Mackenzie Slept Here: A Walking Tour of Dundas.* For the past two years she has administered the short story contest, Creative Keyboards for the Hamilton Arts Council.

Pauline Hewak is a high school English teacher in Hamilton, Ontario. As a child she had some poems published in the *Spectator's* Junior Press Club, and another published in the McMaster student newspaper. For years her writing took the form of letters of complaint and the occasional journal entry. After taking some courses in McMaster's Creative Writing Program she has returned to literary writing.

Lise Lévesque is a Montreal-born writer whose career meandered through the fields of travel, communication, education and mental health. Her present-day challenge, as a director of The Assembly of Francophones of Ontario, is to foment a spirit of democracy within a multi-cultural environment. A graduate of McMaster University's Writing program, she plans to write more fiction than speeches throughout her golden years.

Mary-Eileen McClear is an award-winning storyteller and founder of The Story Barn, a centre which promotes the art of storytelling. She has performed on stages across Canada and in the U.S. Winner of a 2002 Writer's Union of Canada competition for her story "Cows and Robbers", Mary-Eileen can be heard on her recording, "Oh Canada: Strange But True Stories of Early Canada," and on the forthcoming "Voices in the Trees."

Todd McKinstry lives, works and writes in Hamilton, Ontario. Having reached a point in life where he needed to start planning for his retirement before he'd ever really decided what he wanted to do for a living, he took up writing. He is actively at work on his first novel and a book of short stories.

Waheed Rabbani is a historical fiction author living in Grimsby. He was born in India and completed his university education in the UK and Canada. An engineer by profession, Waheed's other love is English literature. He obtained a Certificate in Creative Writing from McMaster University. Waheed's historical novel, Doctor Margaret's Sea Chest, published by Youwriteon-Legend Press UK, is available in print and on line, in bookstores or through Apple iBooks. It's the first book in his Azadi Trilogy. (http://home.cogeco.ca/~wrabbani)

Bernadette Rule is the author of seven collections of poetry, most recently *The Literate Thief* (Larkspur Press, 2006). Larkspur will release another volume of her poetry in 2013. Rule edited Frederick Gower Turnbull's *Remember Me to Everybody: Letters from India, 1945 to 1949* (West Meadow Press, 1996), and hosts Art Waves, an arts-interview radio program, podcast at archive.org/details/artwaves.

Jean Ryan was born in Brooklyn when New York had three major league baseball teams. She moved to Canada in 1971. Upon completing McMaster University's Certificate in Creative Writing in 2008, she received the Award for Academic Excellence. Her memberships include the Storytellers of Canada/Conteurs du Canada, the National Storytelling Network (US) and the Transformative Language Arts Network.

Judy Pollard Smith's articles, travel pieces, book reviews and short stories have appeared in *The Globe And Mail, The National Post, The Hamilton Spectator*, in British magazinesand in the literary magazine *Room*. Other publications include several articles andworkbooks for ESL teachers. Her essays have been read on CBC Radio One. She was awarded Britain's 2012 Lady Violet Astor Rosebowl Award for her article, "Downsizing is a Huge Step" (*Globe & Mail*, Aug. 25, 2011).

The honour was bestowed by The Society Of Women Writers and Journalists.

Richard Van Holst is a research assistant at Redeemer University College in Ancaster, Ontario. His duties allow him to dabble in many of his favourite disciplines, such as literature, history and theology. When he is not working he enjoys reading, listening to classical music, watching a wide variety of films, and of course, writing.

Michelle Ward-Kantor is a mother and part-time elementary teacher who has also worked as a technical writer/editor and secretary. She has won an award for song lyrics and a merit award for technical communication, and has had work published in *Mainstreet, The Prairie Journal, Still Point Arts Quarterly*,and *Stone Voices*. Her work has also appeared online at www.stepawaymagazine.com, www.thewriters-blockmagazine.ca and www.leaplocal.org.

Carol Leigh Wehking has been writing since her childhood: fiction, poetry, essays, and articles. She has for the last couple of decades been a professional storyteller, and though some of her work has been published in newspapers and periodicals, most of her recent writing has reached the public through her performances. She is deeply interested in exploring the stories of real women who chose lives out of the ordinary, and Annie Edson Taylor is one of these. Carol Leigh is a Quaker, has two grown children, and lives in Cambridge, Ontario, with her partner.